Travel Back To Me

Travel Back To Me

Coral Navarro

Library of Congress Control Number:		2011926448
ISBN:	Softcover	978-1-6176-4863-2
	Ebook	978-1-6176-4862-5

To order additional copies of this book, contact:
Palibrio
1-877-407-5847
www.Palibrio.com
ordenes@palibrio.com
338619

CHAPTER I

Erika couldn't curb her enthusiasm; she knew she was at the verge of something that was going to change the direction of her project. When her team knew about it . . . She thought and a smile formed in her lips. Of course, that would have to wait until Monday. Just 'cause she was a workaholic and didn't have a life, didn't mean that the others in her team wouldn't. Sundays were the day when all of them rested usually after a Saturday night excursion in the case of the single people. Married people generally spent the day with their families. They were working Saturdays lately because the project was extremely important, but Erika let them rest on Sundays, after all, they did have lives.

John is going to die when he hears what I have found! Erika thought again, her eyes brilliant with excitement, her mouth slightly open because her breathing was a little faster than usual. *I can't wait to tell him, but I'm not gonna call him today. He must be sleeping after one of his wild nights with some bimbo he must've picked up in a joint. That John!* She moved her head from side to side thinking about him and smiling with a mischievous smile. She loved him as if he were her brother, although there was nothing brotherly about John. His six two feet height with that lean but muscular body and that handsome face with those blue eyes could fool anybody into thinking he was only a pretty boy and that he wasn't that smart. But he was, he was a math genius and he and Erika made a good team. He had tried in the beginning to hit on her. But she had made clear that they worked together and a personal relation between them was not what she wanted. So he had shrugged and smiled and went on with his job and they had built a strong friendship. They worked well together, complementing each other and enjoying working in the project. Erika shook her head now, so she could concentrate on what she was doing. She needed to focus to set the coordinates exactly right; a minimal margin was all it took to create a whole different situation.

The lab was deserted except for her and she wanted to make sure nothing was going to happen other than for what she was trying to do. The only people in the building were the security guards and they were not a great help in the experiments. *Okay,* Erika took a deep breath. *Let's do it. Let's set the coordinates, adjust the controls.* She keyed the computer keys in order to get the right coordinates, pressed enter, looked at the screen to check if what was in display was what she had intended for. The computer was running numbers rapidly in the screen. The screen was black except for the light of the numbers that illuminated her face. *Perfect! The computer is running the program smoothly now. I knew it. I knew there was something in the program.* She thought and she wringed her hands in a satisfaction gesture. *Now let's see what we can try . . . hummm, I don't have a sample here.* She frowned in deep thinking. *What can I send, what can I send . . . Maybe my shoe . . . No! And then if it doesn't work I'll have to go back home in one shoe. A pencil maybe, nope, too small.* She turned her head slowly looking around the lab, with a thoughtful expression. *I know, my calculator! It's an electronic device, it might work. Although I hate to give away my calculator. No, it will be all right, I fixed it, I fixed the problem, so my calculator will be fine. Yes, let's do it.*

She took the calculator and went toward the hexagonal glass chamber. It wasn't really glass, it was more like a mixture between glass and a polymer that gave it the transparent quality but also the durable and resistant qualities to endure the high energies that went on inside. The chamber was the size of a small room, 5 x 5 x 6.5 feet^3.

Erika pressed the buttons on a side console and one glass door opened with a low humming sound. She got inside and ducked to put the calculator on a cushioned pad in the center of the room. At that precise moment, the glass door started to close. When Erika turned around to see what was happening, she stifled a cry of horror. She saw with wide eyes that the door was shutting. There was nothing she could do. She knew that the door had an automatic system of closure and nothing could prevent it from closing. Nevertheless, she stood up as quickly as she could and with both her arms extended toward the door, she tried to push it open. There was still a little space between the door and the other glass panels. Nothing. The door finished closing with a low click. Horror struck as she realized that she was locked in the chamber. *Okay! Easy now. Think! What can you do? Wait, sit here and wait. And then tomorrow, bear all the jokes from my team. If I at least had my cell phone . . . I could call John. He would have the time of his life when he saw me locked down in here.* But her cell phone was on the computer desk beside her purse. *Okay, no cell at hand, then . . . wait.* Suddenly, a set of lights over her head started flashing and immediately afterwards, another set in the floor around the chamber inner radius started flashing too. *What? No, this can't be. No. Oh, my God! The chamber is on. The chamber is activated. I'm going to die! Or . . . I'm going to be the first teleported person in history . . .* The scientific voice inside her head said. With a gesture that meant there's nothing to be done now, Erika took a fall on the floor and braced herself for what was coming, taking a fetal position but with her head securely held between her arms and her eyes pointing to the floor firmly shut. At that moment, a humming and hollow sound was heard and all the lights glowed with an incandescent light. Erika braced herself even stronger and waited. The wait was not long, almost instantaneously she felt as if she was dispersing into the universe. A strange feeling ran through her body or one could say her mind because there was no body left, and for the tiniest time she felt one with the universe and she saw the light . . .

CHAPTER II

Erika opened her eyes, numb and dizzied for a moment. She blinked several times to focus her sight. Her feeling sense came a bit later. Now she felt as if she were on a hard surface. *Strange,* she thought, *if I am alive, this does not feel as the twin chamber in the other laboratory. This feels like . . .* Something itchy was inside her nose. She moved her head to make it go away and the movement made her sneeze. She then lifted her head a little and breathed. A small cloud of dust rose making her cough. *Dirt? This is dirt? Soil! It appears to be soil . . . and plants! Where am I?* She lifted her head a little higher and the sounds came. A thumping on the floor, screams, a thunder noise like . . . *Am I hearing shots?* Erika started to get up from the floor and slowly, because she still felt kind of disoriented, turned around. Her eyes opened wide with surprise. She couldn't believe her eyes. All around her a flat prairie scene spread everywhere. She could see a mountain range in the distance far away. *Wha . . . ?*

Suddenly, she felt a thump and a strong pain around her waist, and she felt herself lifted in the air. She felt another pain in her stomach area as she was indelicately thrown onto something hard and in motion. Something was moving. She tried to lift her head to look, but the movement was so rough that all she could do was stay as still as her position let her and look down at something brown, hairy or she should say furry. *A horse?* She wondered. She was starting to feel giddy and looked at the floor. Big mistake! The blurry soil made her feel nauseated and she tasted the acrid flavor of vomit in her mouth. She was getting dizzier by the minute. She tried to close her eyes but it was worst, so she opened them again and tried to keep them fix to something, which was very hard with the jumping movement she was been subjected to. *God, when is this going to end? Am I dead? Am I in hell?* She was distracted for a moment with these thoughts, so she didn't realize the movement was slowing down until it reached a stop. She felt someone reaching up to her blouse and dragging her off the horse. She found herself standing on the floor a minute later. Her shaky legs were hardly trying to do the job. She took a deep breath trying to stabilize herself and lifted her head.

-What the hell were you doing down there in the middle of the battle, boy? A man yelled at her.

Erika slowly lifted her head a bit more, she was still wobbly, to look at this strange man that was yelling at her. In her scan up she could see that he carried cowboy boots or what seemed like it. Dirty pants with something leathery on his legs, like John Wayne, she thought and a smile emerged on her lips. A pair of guns in every side of him, what looked like a shirt and a hat? Her smile immediately faded as she saw the deep frown that darkened the man's face.

-Are you a woman? What the hell are those clothes you're wearing and what were you doing there? He continued shouting.

-Which one do you want me to answer first? She asked, her voice sounded a little hoarse.

-What? The man looked startled just for a minute.

-I said, which one of the three questions do you want me to answer first? I can't answer them all at the same time.

The man looked at her with an incredulous expression on his face. Then, he turned around and yelled at a boy that was walking by at that moment. –Soldier, take this . . . woman –he hesitated for a moment before saying "woman"—and keep her inside the tent. I'll talk to her when I'm back. Give her some water, she seems like she is going to faint at any moment.

He turned back, got on his horse in one swift movement, and left at a gallop.

She stayed there looking at him with a thoughtful expression. *Who was that? Where am I, indeed?* She was taken out of her thoughts by a shy:—Ma'am?

She turned around and looked at the boy. The man had called him a soldier, but he was not more than a boy. Fifteen? Sixteen maybe? Seventeen years old at the most. He couldn't be a soldier. But he was dressed like one or what it looked like one. His was a uniform she had never seen. The boy was standing there with a wary look in his eyes, waiting for her. She sighed and followed him. He led her toward what looked like a big cloth spread over some posts, the tent. Inside, there were some men in uniform, strange unknown uniforms, leaned over a map, apparently, on a small wooden table. –Who's that? An older man asked casting a quick glance in her direction.

-Josh brought her, he told me to keep her here until he is back. The soldier boy answered.

-I see. Well, make sure she stays out of the way and see to her. The old man said back without uttering one word to her and resumed his discussion with the other men. *How rude!* Erika thought. She was too weary to care though.

-Yes, sir. The soldier addressed her again.—Ma'am? Would you like some water? He had turned to face her now and indicated a camp bed by the tent wall.—You can sit there while you wait, I'll bring you some water.

Erika nodded and sat on the small bed. She was dirty, sweaty, dizzy, and nauseated, besides being exhausted as if she had traveled a long time. She looked around and her eyes stopped at the men who were leaning at the table talking about the best strategy to attack. Attack whom? What war was this? They certainly didn't look like current soldiers. And the guy who brought her here, he was in a horse for God's sake! Erika tried to lean against the wall, but it was cloth and didn't support her, so she stayed seated with her arms on her knees looking at the men. Their uniforms were familiar but she was certain that no one wore those uniforms nowadays. A word that one of the men said caught her attention. *Of course!* She thought. *They are re-enacting a battle. Somehow I fell in one of the South States where they still re-enact the secession war battles. Not exactly what I had planned. But that means it worked! The teleportation chamber worked!* The soldier boy came back with a canteen and offered it to her. Erika took the canteen and thanked the boy. She drank for a while, and then cleaning her mouth with the back of her hand asked the boy. –Hey, is this a re-enactment of one of the secession battles?

The boy stared at her with a blank look.—What ma'am?

-A re-enactment battle. Is this one of them? *Why they had to bring boys to these things?* She thought annoyed.

-I'm sorry ma'am, I don't understand what you are asking, a *Reenaktment* battle? What battle would that be? What Indian name is that?

-What? Indian name? What do you mean Indian? Where are we? Erika asked taken aback.

-You don't know ma'am? The boy's eyes seemed like they were going to pop out of their orbits. –Are you feeling all right? Perhaps it would be better if you rest for a while until Josh comes back. He said politely.

-Josh? Is that the man's name? The one who brought me here?

-Yes, ma'am. Everybody around here knows Josh. He's the best. The boy's face showed the admiration he felt for the guy.

-Soldier! Let the lady rest. She looks like she needs it. The old man scolded the young soldier.

-Yes, sir. Rest now ma'am. I'm sure Josh will answer all your doubts when he comes back. He turned around and quickly left the tent not wanting another scolding.

-But . . . Erika tried to say, but the boy was already gone and the men there weren't paying much attention to her. They were deeply in discussion again.

Well, I may as well rest for a while. This is certainly very weird. Erika laid down on the bed and closed her eyes. Without realizing it, she fell asleep.

CHAPTER III

Someone was shaking her. –Hey, lady. Wake up. Wake up lady, we have to move.

-Wha . . . ? Erika blinked her eyes several times trying to focus. *Why is someone waking me up in my bed? John? No, that's not John's voice. Is there something wrong? Is the building on fire?* She suddenly sat up in the bed and looked around disoriented. Her memories were slowly coming back. She looked up at the man standing beside her. Josh. The man that had brought her here. *Here! What is here? Where is here? Where am I?* Josh interrupted her thoughts.

-Come on, lady. We need to go. We're going back to the fort. There's nothing else we can do here. He was speaking and at the same time grabbing her arm and forcing her to stand.

-The fort? She asked confused.

-Yes, the fort. Let's go. He said impatiently looking at her with a frown glance. His hand was gripping her arm tightly and he was hurting her.

-But . . . where are we? She asked again, still puzzled.

-You don't know? Did you bang your head and lose your memory or something? He shook her lightly.

-I . . . No, I did not lose my memory. It is completely fine. She said offended. –And you're hurting me! Please let go of my arm!

Startled, as if he hadn't realized he was holding her firmly, he released her.—Well, then stop asking stupid questions and come. We have to leave now, before those damn Indians come back.

-Indians? Did you say Indians? That is not a very polite way to call the native-Americans, you know? And why would be any problem if they come? Josh looked at her as if she had lost her mind. He breathed deeply to calm himself and told her kindlier,—Look lady . . .

-Banner, Erika Banner. Doctor Erika Banner actually. She interrupted him.

-What? He asked incredulously looking at her with a murderous look now. His emotions clearly changing on his face. One could say he was getting exasperated. He didn't seem to be in a very good mood either and he seemed to have a temper, actually. Well, neither was she in a good mood. She was dirty, sweaty, tired, and confused.

-I said that my name is . . .

-I heard the first time –He rudely interrupted her.—Are you a doctor? A medical doctor? Disbelief showing on his attitude.

-No, I'm not a medical doctor. She said affronted by his tone and his expression. –I'm a doctor in

Quantum Physics if you must know. I've a PhD. She finished snubbed and raised her nose a few inches. People that worked with her respected her greatly because they knew how smart and devoted she was to her work, but those who didn't know her sometimes made the mistake to underestimate her. Like this guy here. *A cowboy for God's sake!* She thought scornfully.

-A what? Look, lady or Doctor Banner or whoever the hell you are, I don't have time for this. You either come with me to the fort or you stay here in this deserted place at the mercy of those goddamn Indians. You decide. But make it quick because I'm leaving right now. He was still frowning and he was getting more irritated by the minute.

Erika was utterly confused, she wasn't used to this type of treatment, and she needed to know what had happened, where she was, and how she was going to go back to NASA. But that thing he had said about a deserted place and staying all alone and Indians . . . Indians? Why he kept calling them Indians? That was not right, her friend John would break the guy's nose just for calling him that. Not that he and any of his people would not call themselves Indians. But one thing was for a native-American called himself that and other thing that a white guy said it. People were very careful about labeling people on account of their race nowadays. They were trying to respect everyone's heritage and diversity and get along, without all of the race nonsense of the past. People were people, all made the same and the important thing was to respect the different cultures but without segregation, just embracing the differences and reinforcing the similarities. Josh

was standing there looking at her as if he thought
she wasn't worth the trouble, so snapping out of her
thoughts she quickly made a decision.

-I'll go with you. But I need someone to answer
my questions. I need someone to at least give me
directions to go back home. She said trying to sound
reasonable but firm, so this Neanderthal cowboy
would calm down. She was used to speak authoritative
and she was used to people obeying her without
hesitation. This man however, appeared to be used
to have his way.

-I'll give you directions and all the information I can
as soon as we are safely back. Josh answered her less
harshly this time. He seemed to notice the effort
she had made to speak to him in a controlled way.
Somehow he found it funny so a semi smile formed
on his lips.

They went out of the tent, as some soldiers started
to take it down. She stopped immediately on her
feet. –Where are the cars? All she could see were
horses everywhere. And groups of soldiers that were
preparing to leave on foot.

-Carts? He said misunderstanding what she
said.—There are no carts or wagons, just horses. And
not enough horses for that matter, I'm afraid that
you'll have to ride with me.

-No, I'm afraid you didn't understand me, I meant
cars as in automobiles. Where are they? I don't know
how to ride a horse and I don't think I like it after
this morning.

-Look, lady . . . Miss or Mrs. Banner –he corrected
when he saw she was going to interrupt him again—I
don't know what those things you just said are. Horses

are all there is, either you ride with me or you walk, your choice.

Erika saw he was starting to get exasperated again and she didn't feel like getting into an argument, she was too tired, so she sighed and conceded. –Okay, but you'll have to help me get on the horse. I don't know how.

-You have never ridden a horse? Lady, where have you been?

At a lab, she thought but didn't say anything aloud. He whistled and a brown horse that was grazing nearby approached them. He helped her getting on the horse. It was a good thing that she was wearing jeans, which were resistant and somewhat protected her from the saddle. Then, in a quick and gracious move he got on the horse behind her. He took the bridle with one hand. He put his other arm around Erika's waist and positioned her more comfortable on the saddle, moving her closer to him. Too close in Erika's opinion. She fidgeted trying to separate herself a little, but he tightened his arm around her and pulled her against his body, like glue. She tried to move away again and he said:—Hey, lady, don't wiggle like that, stay as I placed you. We are good for a five hour riding and this is the more comfortable position for both of us. I'm sorry if my closeness offends your sensibility but there is nothing that I can do. And if you keep moving it's going to get more uncomfortable.

-Five hour riding? She asked in dismay.—You're kidding, right? I don't think I can't stand five hours on a horse. And it would be a lot more comfortable if you didn't have your hard penis pressed against my

butt. *God! Did she say that aloud?* She closed her mouth
too embarrassed to continue and felt how her ears
were burning.

Josh was startled for a minute because of what
she had just said and suddenly started to laugh,
throwing his head backwards. –I give you this, lady.
You are the strangest, most daring woman I have ever
crossed paths with. No self-respected woman I know
would have said that. Unless it was a hooker and you
don't strike me as one. Then again, those odd clothes
you wear . . . He ran his gaze from her head to her
toe,—do you work in a circus by any chance? He was
amused now.

-What? How dare you? She turned her head toward
him as much as she could and looked furiously at
him.—Of course I'm not a hooker. I told you I'm a
PhD in Quantum . . .

-Physics, yes I heard you the first time. I just don't
have the faintest idea what that is.

-And what about my clothes? She continued as if she
hadn't heard him.—This jean, she indicated her
pants,—is very comfortable for the lab and today is
Sunday, so I don't need to dress up . . .

-Yep, the fabric of those pants seems to be resistant
and they stick to you as a second skin. Not a very
ladylike thing to wear, though. But I have to reckon at
least you can ride astride. It would have been a bitch
to ride with you sideways. Erika started to answer him
but then something occurred to her and she kept her
mouth shut deep in thought. A wild idea was forming
in her mind and she needed to analyze it. She usually
thought before acting or talking, though today she
just wasn't herself. Maybe the teleporting had altered

her in some way or maybe she was just tired and confused and uncomfortable on this horse.

They rode silently for a while. They were riding along a line of soldiers on horses. There were three lines of horses in total and soldiers walking ahead, by the sides, and behind. They were riding in one of the outer lines. Erika could feel the hardness of his body stuck to her, his arm around her waist, while his other hand was leisurely holding the reins. His legs were touching her legs with every motion of the horse. She could also still feel his hardness against her buttocks. Did riding a horse always arouse men? Or did it have to be with them riding so close to each other? This was getting more awkward by the minute and there was nothing that she could do to avoid it, unless she was willing to walk. And she wasn't. As uncomfortable as riding with him was, walking seemed even worse. She would bear his hardness instead of the walking. To get her mind off that line of thought she asked him:—So, Mr . . . .

-Josh, he interrupted her,—just Josh.

-Okay, so Josh, what is the name of the fort we are heading for?

-Fort Crawford.

-Fort Crawford? Where is that located? She had never heard of a place called like that. Not that she have ever cared for geography much.

-By the Mississippi River.

-The Mississippi River? Oh, my God! Okay, the Mississippi River is very large. You'll have to be more specific. Where exactly? Minnesota, Wisconsin, Iowa, Illinois, Missouri, Tennessee, Louisiana? She recited. She knew all the States the Mississippi River crossed, because this magnificent river had always caught her attention, even if she didn't know other geography stuff.

-We are north of Illinois.

-You mean we are in Wisconsin? She asked him taken aback. She tried to picture the US map in her head. How the hell had she ended up in Wisconsin when she had been intended for the West Coast?

-No, we're in Michigan territory, to the west is the Missouri territory, where do you think you are?

-California!

-California? Lady, we are far from California. Are you Mexican or Spaniard? Now it was his turn to be surprised. –You don't look Mexican, as for Spaniard . . . Your English is good, though I must reckon you do speak queer. I can't exactly point out what it is but . . .

-Look, Erika tried to turn her head to look at him.—This is a very uncomfortable way to keep a conversation. She said frustrated.—I would like to look at you when I'm talking to you. Just let go of me for a minute.

-Lady, what are . . . ? Josh started to ask, but she took him by surprise and grabbing his hand, pushed it away. She turned and put a hand on his shoulder as leverage, passing her leg carefully and with great effort over the horse's head until she was seated sideways. She stopped momentarily to catch her breath.

-Hey, lady! You're gonna make us fall off the horse. Josh tightened his grip on the horse's reins to avoid it.

-Not lady. Erika said sounding out of breath because of the effort she was making to turn around.—If you're not going to address me as Dr. Banner or Miss Banner, call me Erika. And hold me and don't let me fall. Now she put both her arms around Josh's neck and passed the other leg bending it between them until she was astride but facing him. Josh had to hold the reins with both hands and keep his arms around her so they wouldn't fall while she was doing the turning. He now held her with one arm and pulled her toward him again to better accommodate her on his lap. Her legs had ended over Josh's legs after the movement, so his hard bulge was positioned against her crotch and she gasped when she felt his hardness. Josh lifted an eyebrow and glanced at her. –You know . . . Erika, this is not doing any good to your reputation. And I'm not marrying you for it in case you got any ideas. He commented ironically but with a husky voice.

She took a deep breath trying to ignore the warm feeling that was starting to spread over her body.—The hell with my reputation. And I'm not looking for a husband. She answered fiercely trying to offset her feelings. Josh couldn't help but laugh again. Some of the soldiers around were looking at them with wide eyes at this unconventional riding. When Josh tired of laughing he found Erika looking at him with an enraged face.—What?

-This is *so* not funny. Tell me again. She found, nonetheless, that it was difficult for her to concentrate on what they were talking about with his hard on just in between her legs. This was a very intimate position that the up and down movement of the horse didn't help. But she mentally waved away that reaction and tried to focus. –What do you mean by Michigan Territory? The US is divided in states not territories. A cold sweat was going down her back as she waited for him to answer for a suspicion was forming in her mind.

-Lad . . . I mean Erika . . . I don't know your game or if the Indians kidnapped you and that drove you nuts but we are in Michigan Territory. The states are Illinois, Indiana, Tennessee, Mississippi, Louisiana, and those to the east.

-What year is this? Erika asked closing her eyes.

-Are you playing with me? Josh asked with a frown. He was getting upset or maybe that was not the right word to describe him, annoyed or mad, was probably a better word.

-Please, Josh, just answer the question. She kept her eyes closed and held her breath. Josh could see real distress in her face, so he softened his tone.

-We are in 1821, July 15.

She let the air slowly get out of her and she said with a small voice. –Oh my God! That can't be. That is impossible. I could not. I wouldn't. Suddenly all the color fade out of her face and she went as pale as a ghost. She felt so dizzy that she started to slide down. If it weren't for the fact that Josh had his two arms around her while he was holding the reins, she would have slid down all the way to the ground.

-Erika? Are you all right? You look like you've seen a ghost. He tightened his arms around her and pushed her more against him. –There, lean on me. I've got you. Don't worry; it's not far now. We're getting closer to the fort. His voice was softer now, the man reacting naturally to a woman in need.

Erika leaned on Josh's body as told; her arms were hanging at her sides. She closed her eyes and said:—Thank you Josh, I'll be fine in a minute.

-It's all right, I don't mind at all. Josh replied with a husky voice. This riding was affecting both of them in more than one way.

-Yeah, I can feel *that*. Erika said with a strangle voice. However, she felt so weak that she didn't move back.

-Sleep a little if you can. I'll hold you. I won't let you fall. He grabbed the reins with one hand and put the other one around Erika's back holding her close against him. They rode two more hours while Erika dozed. She could tell because, funny thing, her wristwatch was working. *My wristwatch!* She thought suddenly completely awake. *I'll have to hide it and anything that is not been invented or discovered by now. You mean as your Levi's and your Nike's and your rubber band. Wait, watches have already been invented. Yeah, but not like the one you carry.* Hers was a water resistant Citizen watch with alarm, perpetual calendar, 1/20-second chronograph, 12/24-hour time, dual time, date display, luminous hands and markers, and unidirectional rotating bezel. *Yeah, so I like men's watches, they have more features than women's watches.* She thought speaking with herself. Carefully, she opened the watch bracelet and surreptitiously slid it inside her pants front pocket. Josh felt her movement. –You're awake. We're approaching the fort now. You can get some dinner and rest.

-Ah, Josh. I need to tell you something. But I would rather it was kept between us. She said carefully lifting her head to look at him. She studied his hard features trying to decide whether he could take it. *Yeah, he can.* She thought. His eyes had a smart look, he was a little rough and coarse and he absolutely needed a shaving and a bath but he definitely looked intelligent.

-Yeah, we have to talk. You need to tell me what you were doing in the middle of the prairie while there was a battle going on. But we'll do it tomorrow. We are both tired.

They arrived at the fort, which consisted of square log work with two blockhouses and diagonal angles. The buildings were erected with square logs of about 8-10 inches square and the barracks for the officers and men formed three squares of the fort, the doctor's office, guardhouse, the artificer's shop, and some small houses formed the fourth. The logs were laid so close as to them, which made the fort a complete defense against small arms. Most people there were soldiers, but there were some civilians, including a few women and children. There were also some houses outside the fort scattered in the proximity. Josh took Erika to one of the small houses inside the fort. A young woman was there.

-Good evening Anna, how are you today? Josh asked the young woman respectfully touching his hat with his hand. She was probably 25 years old at the most, with blond hair and clear blue eyes. She was pretty, delicate, and small.

-I am fine Josh, how are you today? She answered a little bit wary.

-We did fine, but we had to come back.

-Did many . . . Indians die? She asked with a subdued voice. Erika thought she noticed certain hesitation before the word "Indians".

-No, not many. Just two of them and one of ours.

-The chief?

-No, not the chief. Sorry Anna. Erika saw how Josh's voice became harder and how he tensed his jaw, however his behavior toward this woman was gentle, almost careful.

-Ah . . . But Erika sensed more relief in that expression than anything else.

-I have a favor to ask of you.

-Of course. Anything that you need. Erika kept studying this woman carefully. Something did not fit in. She seemed tense and not at all accommodating as she was trying to appear.

-This is Dr. Banner, Erika Banner. She needs a place to stay for the night and probably for a while. She will also need some clothes, I think. He deliberately looked her up and down.—As you are here alone I was wondering if you would mind to have her here with you until her situation is solved.

-Of course, by all means. She can stay with me as long as she needs. She smiled, but her smile didn't reach her eyes, which were full of sorrow. She turned now to Erika and extending her hand said:—It is nice to meet you Dr. Banner.

-Please call me Erika. She smiled back taking Anna's hand.

-Well, I'll leave you two alone now. I'll see you tomorrow to have that conversation, Erika. Josh turned and left after saying good-bye to Anna.

-Please come inside. Anna invited Erika to get into her house.

-Thank you. Erika stepped inside the place. It was a small room with a square wooden table that had four simple chairs and a hearth where a small cauldron was being heated. On one of the walls there were some shelves and cupboards and a cabinet with two basins on it. At one side of the room there was a door that Erika assumed it would be the bedroom. *Where was the bathroom? Have they invented the bathroom by 1821? Oh God, don't tell me I have to go somewhere in the wilds.* Erika thought.

-I'm making supper. Are you hungry? Anna asked Erika.

-Actually I am, but I was thinking that I need to use the bathroom first.

-Pardon me. You need to use the what?

Oh man, and I have to be careful with what I say too. Damn. –I mean that I need to take care of some physiological needs. Erika repeated with a gesture.

-Ah, you need to urinate or maybe you need to move your bowels?

-Just the first for now. This was really embarrassing, even between two women. This type of conversation was not something that was socially discussed even nowadays.

-There's a chamber pot in the bedroom. You may use it. Later, I'll show you the outhouse, where we take care of the second business. It's not so bad because there is one for women's use only. *Great!* Erika thought *I'll have to go outside for number two.*

-Thanks. Ah, how do I dispose of the urine? She inquired instead.

-Just throw it out the window.

-Throw it out the window? Erika asked surprised. *Jesus, is this 1821 or the middle ages?*

-It's all right, there is nothing back there. The pot has some clean water in it. I always maintain some in it to keep it from stinking. After you throw out the urine, please use the water in the bucket that is on the corner to rinse it and make sure to leave some water in it.

-I'll do that. Thanks again. Erika went to the bedroom and closed the door. She opened her jeans and quickly took them down; she did the same with her underwear and squatted over the pot. *I wonder where I have to go to do number two.* She thought preoccupied. *What about electricity? They haven't discovered its applications yet. Shit! What a time to travel in time!* She finished and cleaned the pot as Anna had told her. Then she put some water in a washbowl and rinsed her hands. *No soap! I'll have to ask Anna, I'm pretty sure they use soap by now.*

-Ready. Erika said, coming out of the bedroom. –I did what you told me and I rinsed my hands on the washbowl, I didn't throw that water, though.

-It's all right. Oh, there is no soap in there. I used it all today. Here, and she took a homemade soap out of a wooden shelf. –Um, it seems I'll have to make more tomorrow or the day after. I'm running out of it.

Erika took the soap and washed her hands again, she also washed her face and this time she threw away the water.

-You would probably like to take a bath to freshen up, the temperature is rising now the summer is coming, but supper is ready and I think it is best if we eat while is warm. Anna told Erika when she came out of the bedroom again.

-A bath would be wonderful, but to tell you the truth I'm starving. I haven't had anything to eat since this morning and all I ate was coffee and a cracker.

-Let's eat then. Anna served the meat stew she had prepared in two metal bowls.

They ate in silence until Anna broke it to ask. –I have never known a woman doctor.

-I am not a medical doctor.

-Is there any other kind of doctor? Anna looked at Erika in surprise.

-Well, it's kind of hard to explain, but I studied a lot and after you study for some years, they give you a degree that is called a philosophical doctorate. At the expression of astonishment in Anna's face, Erika continued:—Never mind, it's something I couldn't use here anyway. So, I think it would be better if you don't say anything to anybody about it. I mean, I would appreciate it if you wouldn't. I don't want people thinking that I can treat or heal them.

-Don't worry. I don't talk to anybody here, so your secret or whatever it is, is safe with me. Anna spoke with a soft low voice and continued eating.

-You don't? Why not? Erika was curious. Anna was a beautiful woman. Surely there was some guy who was courting her or whatever they called it in those days.

-Well, you may as well know it. So, if you want to go to another place to stay, you can do it right now. None of the respectable women in here would want anything to do with the Indian's whore. And most of the men, too. Anna finished defiantly rising her chin. Her lower lip was trembling a little but her eyes shone with a light.

-What? Erika's mouth fell open and she spat the food out. –The Indian's whore? Boy, what's with the Native-Americans here? She took a napkin Anna had put on her place and cleaned herself and the mess she'd done on the table as best she could.

-Yes,—Anna continued—a Dakota tribe from the Sioux kidnapped me. It's a long story. Now they, the army I mean, rescued me back. But because I was living with an . . . Indian, they think I am a whore. So they call me the Indian's whore. You may leave if you want to, otherwise your reputation may suffer too. I don't know what Josh was thinking when he brought you here with me. Erika was stunned.

-Wait, I am not going anywhere, unless you want me to, in which case I will. I know I'm probably a nuisance to you, but I don't think you are a whore because some man forced you to sleep with him, Indian or no Indian.

-You don't understand –and now Anna's face had become hard and defiant—I wasn't *forced* to sleep with him, I did it because I wanted to. I have a son with him. She explained.

-You do? That's wonderful! I mean, that you have a son . . . Wait, if you weren't forced to be with him, why are you here?

-Because Josh and the army were doing a reconnaissance and I was alone in the river washing clothes. They saw me there and they thought I needed rescuing. They didn't even bother to ask. They saw a white woman and they just automatically thought I wanted to come back. She finished bitterly.

-Why don't you leave and go back to your man?

-Because I don't know the land, I would get lost and besides the Dakota move a lot, because the army is pushing them out of their lands. I wouldn't know where to go. Anyway, after they brought me here, some Indians attacked them in another reconnaissance.

I think is them, the Dakota. Since then, I've been worried sick that they may kill Chetan.

-Chetan?

-That's his name. My man's name, as you put it. He is my husband really. We had a ceremony. It's not a ceremony that folks here would consider real but to me is. The expressions on her face changed from pride to happiness to anger.

-Anna . . . This must be very hard for you, being separated from your son and your husband. I'm so sorry. I really hope that you find the way to go back to them.

-So, you don't mind? That I lived with a Sioux? That I want to go back with him and leave my people behind?

-Where I come from, we think differently. We don't judge people because of their race but because of their actions. I don't think you have anything to be ashamed of. I really would like to help you going back to your people, 'cause that's truly what they are.

-Thank you. You certainly are different. Actually, you do not look like a local woman. Your clothes, I have never seen a woman wearing men's clothes, although those are not exactly like the local men's. Where are you from? How did you end up here at Fort Crawford?

-I . . . I don't know exactly what happened. I can't remember. All I know is that one minute I was working and the next I was in the middle of nowhere. Josh found me and brought me here.

Well, that was not exactly the truth but it wasn't a lie either. Erika didn't think it was a good idea to tell people from the XIX century that she was from the

XXI century and that she had been teleported into the past by mistake. But she needed to tell someone so she could get help to go back to her time and she thought that one person could be Josh. Or at least she hoped that he rose to the occasion.

-You must be tired. I'm afraid I have only one small bed.

-It's okay. If you have some blankets, I can sleep on the floor. I really am tired. I woke up very early this morning, it seems like two centuries had passed since then. *Literally!*

-I can lend you a nightgown if you'd like. I can lend you a dress too for tomorrow, so you can wash your clothes. I don't have many clothes though in the time I've been here I have sewn a couple of dresses and other pieces of clothing.

-I'd appreciate it. I lost all my belongings. That was not exactly true either, but again what could she possibly say?—If you don't mind though, I'd prefer a blouse if you have one. My jeans . . . pants I mean, can endure some more wearing. Pants are more comfortable than dresses to me.

-Oh, all right. Anna went in search of the garments and blankets for Erika. At the bed foot they extended three blankets and a pillow, so Erika was as comfortable as possible under the circumstances. Anna also gave Erika an additional blanket to cover herself. –Maybe I should tell someone to bring some hay to put under the blankets so it's more cushioned.

-No, Anna, don't bother. I can sleep just fine on the floor. That was another lie. She never ever went camping because she didn't like the discomfort of sleeping on the floor. She loved her soft, big, and luxurious bed, but she didn't want to cause any more trouble than necessary.

She started to undress as she usually did. She wouldn't normally take off her clothes in the presence of another person, but as both were female she thought it wouldn't be a problem. She was mistaken. Anna was staring at her flabbergasted. Erika had completely forgot about her delicate lace underwear. It was black and though it wasn't a thong, it was pretty small for the XIX century standards. Erika was probably lucky that Anna had been living with Native-Americans and she was used to different customs in clothing, otherwise she would have probably thrown her out. Anna gasped and Erika raised her head to look at her. She immediately realized her mistake. *Damn it! I forgot about my underwear.* –Ah . . . I know what you must be thinking. These are my summer underwear clothes. See, where I live is very warm and we need to wear light clothing.

Anna looked intensely at Erika for a moment. Then, she turned and began to undress herself. –I guess that must be a lot more comfortable than this. She commented indicating her drawers, camisole, corset, and petticoat.—When I lived with the Sioux my clothes were much more simple. I wore a dress, leggings, and moccasins; those are the shoes they wear. Sometimes, at summer time I wore only a skirt. I was very embarrassed and self-conscious at first because my breasts were bare, but I found out quickly that for the Sioux the human body is something natural. So, I went on doing what the Sioux women did. Anna said matter-of-factly and shrugged.

It was Erika's turn to be open-mouthed. Okay, so maybe this woman was ahead of her time. She hadn't fainted or screamed or called her a whore and threw her out of her house. She had seen her two-centuries-ahead-underwear and she had commented about the comfortableness of clothes and her life with the Sioux. This could be an interesting time after all, at least until she found the way to go back. She said good night to Anna and prepared herself to sleep. She surreptitiously took her wristwatch out of her jeans pocket and looked at the time. *That couldn't be the time. Seven thirty? It was still so early and they were going to bed? What a waste of time.* Erika went to bed at eleven everyday, tired but satisfied with a well-spent working day. Today, with the sun still in the sky, she was already in bed. Maybe she could get up and think about what could have gone wrong at the lab for it to happen. Maybe if she . . .

CHAPTER IV

Erika slowly opened her eyes. She had had a dream where she had been working at the lab and she had traveled through time back to 1821. Boy, was her bed hard today! She turned to her side trying to go back to sleep. Her clock alarm hadn't gone off yet, so it was still probably too early to get up. She turned again to the other side trying to find a more comfortable position and her legs got tangled with the fabric of her nightgown. *Wait! I don't wear nightgowns. I don't own nightgowns! My pajamas are soft, smooth, and delicate. It wasn't a dream!* She jerked up in a sudden movement wide-awake now. She looked around but all she could see were shadows and dark forms. Slowly, her eyes became accustomed to the darkness and she was able to make out the bed where Anna still slept. Carefully, she took out her watch from under the pillow where she had hidden it last night and saw the time: 5:50 am. She got up from her blankets trying not to make

any noise. She had physiological needs to take care
of. Number one for the time being. She took the
chamber pot and tiptoed out of the bedroom. When
she was ready, she entered the bedroom trying to be
quiet. Anna was waking up. –I'm sorry. Did I wake
you?

-No, I always wake very early. Anna yawned and
smiled.

-Anna, I'm sorry to bother you, but would you tell me
where the bathr . . . I mean the outhouse is?

-Sure, I'll go with you, so you know where it is and we
can keep company to each other. It's a little bit early
and one of the soldiers may be prowling around.
Anna took two pieces of cloth and when she saw
Erika's perplexed expression she explained:—To
wipe us up. We can wash them later if they are not
too dirty afterwards; otherwise you just throw it out.
Yeah! Right! Use it again . . . Erika thought with disgust
imagining the unpleasant task. But all she said to
Anna was—Thanks. Ah Anna . . . where can I take a
bath? I really, really would like to get clean up, I'm all
sticky and dirty.

-Well, in the winter I would use the tub, but in summer
time I usually go to the river, there is a spot that I found
where I wash myself and also wash the clothes. I'll go
with you to take a bath, if you don't mind, after we go to
the outhouse. Let's take some clothes and something
to dry us up. She went to the wooden wardrobe of her
bedroom and took out two big sheets of cloth and
some garments.—Here's a blouse for you . . . . But
I don't have anything remotely similar to your light
underwear. She said in a pensive attitude putting a
finger to her lips.—I know! We can wash the clothes

before we bathe ourselves and that way the garments
will dry up while we bathe. So you can put them back
on. How that sounds? She turned and smiled at Erika.
Erika thought Anna was a resourceful and intelligent
woman and very open-minded for this time. Thank
God for falling into the hands of someone like her!
She smiled back at Anna and said:—I think that's a
great idea, Anna.

-All right, so let's take the soap and a bucket and I
think we are ready to go. Ooops! Sorry for keeping
you! I will lead the way.

They left the house when it was still dark and
walked through the deserted road between the
houses. Anna led the way holding an oil lamp in
front of them. The outhouse was a little far from the
houses, naturally. The smell given off of it was strong
and nauseating. Erika gagged and pinched her nose
making a disgusted face. Anna told her to go first
while she waited. Erika opened the wooden door of a
small room with a deep hole on the ground. She took
a deep breath and trying to hold her breath entered
the outhouse. She hanged up the oil lamp in a kind
of iron hook nailed on the door. She was getting out
of air but she didn't want to breath in. She put a hand
to cover her mouth and nose and breathed into it.
The smell made her sick. Erika emptied her bowels
as soon as she was capable of holding up the feeling
of throwing up and got out of it quickly. She waited
impatiently until Anna was done and couldn't wait
to get as far away from that place as she could. *Jee!
That was disgusting! When did men invent the bathroom
with plumbing?? Wasn't it in this century? Why couldn't
I had jumped in a later time, with running water and a*

kitchen . . . Erika sighed and followed Anna toward the river. *At least she would be clean shortly . . .*

After a fifteen-minute walk they finally arrived to the river shore. By that time the sun had already risen and the budding morning was starting to get warm. The place where Anna had taken them was a shallow stream that branched from the deeper river. It was very conveniently located since it had some bushes that covered most of the place. Erika undressed, putting one of the cloths that Anna had brought around her and firmly holding it by inserting a folded piece inside it. She took her underwear, socks, and blouse with one hand and with the other she took her jeans and shoes, and came out of the bushes where she had gotten in to undress. She got closer to the shore where Anna was waiting and crouched down beside her. Hesitantly she asked Anna:—Could you please tell me how to wash my clothes? I haven't done it in this way before.

Anna looked in surprise at her but didn't comment on such a strange remark and showed her how to do it. –You take one garment and soak it in the water. Then you rub the soap all over it and rub hard the garment until it is clean. Finally, you rinse it in the water until you don't feel the soap anymore. I usually hang it out on a line in a small backyard that I have beside the kitchen but as we are going to bathe afterwards, we'll just put it on the bushes to dry. She smiled at her and continued washing all the garments she had brought that in Erika's opinion was a lot. Erika clumsily started to wash her underwear as told, then her socks and finally her blouse. She left the jeans for another time for two reasons: one because as she had told Anna yesterday, the jeans could stand another day or two. The second reason was because frankly denim fabric is hard and she didn't want to hurt her hands with the primitive soap and the primitive way of washing. She would figure out later how to do it with the minimum damage to her skin. When she was finished, more out of good manners than out of really want to continue doing this physical work, which she didn't like and for which she paid at home, se asked Anna:—Would you like me to help you with one of your garments?

But Anna that had observed Erika's struggle to do a simple chore like that, smartly declined. –No, go ahead and take your bath. I'm almost finished. Take this soap to wash some of that dirt out.

-The hair . . . you wash it also with the soap? Erika asked, thinking about her silky hair, carefully treated with soft shampoos and creams.

-Yes. Sorry I don't have those lotions that some of the girls in cities have.

-It's okay. Erika shrugged and for a moment of hesitation stood there. Then, she thought about what Anna had told her last night that sometimes she was topless among her husband's tribe and taking off the towel stepped into the water.—*Shit!* She said loudly and for a moment was left breathless. The water was cold! She hadn't noticed how much while she washed her clothes.

Anna looked at her, frightened. –What happened?

-Nothing. It's just that the water is colder than I thought. She took a deep breath and stepped deeper into the water. Erika washed herself as fast as she could, soaping her hair and body and rinsing by submerging under the water. Shivering, she got out of the river and took the cloth to dry herself. Her teeth were chattering. She wrapped herself up in the cloth and stayed there. *Oh God! What is this? Why is this happening to me? Am I stuck in this time forever?* Her eyes shone with moisture. *NO!* She screamed mentally at herself. *No. I'm not gonna surrender! I'm going to do everything in my power to go back or die in the attempt! Eh . . . Okay . . . too much drama. But not seriously, I have to find the way to go back to my time. I am not cut out for this. This is not my thing. I cannot do anything here, not now. I . . .*

-Erika? Are you all right? Was the water too cold? I'm sorry. I guess I'm accustomed to cold temperatures. I didn't realize . . . Maybe where you come from is warmer . . . ? Anna was already getting dressed. She had bathed and dried quickly; in the efficient way she did things. She was used to this kind of life. It was the usual life of a pioneer or a farmer in the old and Wild West. It was a hard life, but she didn't ask questions, actually nobody at that time did. That was just the way things were. They lived according to it. Erika snapped out of her thoughts.

-I . . . I'm okay Anna. I'll get dressed. Yes, the water temperature took me by surprise. I didn't expect it to be that cold. I'll get used to it though. She smiled at Anna, who was watching her with a look mix of puzzlement and worry. Erika put on her underwear, which was still wet, but not as much as her socks, though these too Erika put on. She finished dressing with the blouse Anna had lent her and her jean and shoes. They took the rest of the clothes and other garments that Anna had washed and folding them, put them in the bucket they had brought.

By the time they arrived to Anna's house, Erika was starving. Anna offered her some coffee and a piece of bread she had baked the day before with cheese. Erika devoured the bread in a minute and then sat to drink her coffee thinking of what she needed to make her calculations. –Anna . . . Do you have something to write with?

-You mean a quill? No, I'm sorry. My husband can't read and I don't have anybody else to write to, so I haven't taken the time to buy writing instruments. Perhaps Josh or the soldiers could lend you something to write . . . Do you want to write to anyone back home?

-No, not to write to anybody. My letters would not reach them. Not now anyway . . . She said distracted, already deep in her thoughts. –I think I'll go and ask that guy, Josh. See if he has some writing implements to lend me. She was already heading for the door when something occurred to her and she turned to say reluctantly to Anna:—Unless you need me to help you with some chores . . . ?

-No, Erika, thanks. Go ahead. I'll fix lunch. Maybe you can help me later by washing the dishes?

-Sure, Anna. Erika left and walked purposefully toward where Anna had told her she could find Josh. As she was concentrating on the calculations she needed to perform in order to see whether she could do something to go back to her time, she didn't realize the astonished looks she was producing among the men and women that she came across with in the fort. When she reached the military office, she asked for Josh before the astounded look of the soldier there.

-Is something the matter, soldier? Erika could not get over the fact that these soldiers were so young, kids.

-I'm sorry ma'am. The soldier said blushing when he realized he had been staring at the strange woman that wore pants like a man. –I'll go tell Josh. He entered the next room letting the door open, so Erika could see some military men and Josh were deep in discussion. She saw something that caught her attention and without hesitation she went closer to a table next to a wall, where a military artifact rested on.

–Hey lady, don't touch that. A voice called to her. Immediately, Josh was already there beside her. –What are you doing here? I was going to go to Anna's later to have that discussion.

-Good morning to you too. She said with sarcasm. –I came to see if you could lend me some writing instruments. I need to write something down. She said still looking with interest at the strange artifact on the table. It was a kind of model embodying a very basic and rough cannon.

-Writing instruments? Josh asked confused.

-Yeah, a pen, paper, stuff like that.

-You mean a quill? Colonel, do you have a quill, ink, and a notebook for her? Maybe she needs to inform some relative where she is. Josh said turning to face one of the men in the room. Erika raised her head and realized that all the men in the room were looking at her with frowning expressions. They probably didn't appreciate a woman interrupting their war strategies chat. Erika thought with contempt. *The bastards! Who do they think they are? She probably outsmarted all of them in there.*

-Sure Josh, I think that I have one quill and ink over here. Soldier! Get a notebook for the lady. The man addressed as colonel ordered the soldier who had attended her.

-Miss Banner! Erika corrected exasperated. –If you won't call me Dr. Banner at least address me as Miss Banner.

-I beg your pardon? The old colonel had blushed with anger.

-That my name is Erika Banner, Colonel . . .

-MacPherson. Josh intervened. –I'm sorry you have not been properly introduced. Colonel? He said addressing the colonel.—This is Erika Banner. *Doctor* Erika Banner. Not Medical Doctor though. Something different that I can't still understand myself. Josh finished a little cynically.—Dr. Banner, this is Colonel MacPherson.

Erika ignored Josh's sarcasm and nodded politely to the colonel. –Colonel . . .

-Miss Banner . . . The colonel answered with a grunt.

-Here is what you asked for, colonel. The young soldier came back with a notebook.

-Here miss. Take my quill and ink. You can use it as long as you need it. The colonel said reminding his manners for behaving in front of a lady. His voice had softened a little. He held out a quill and a small ink flask towards Erika.

-You've got to be kidding me! Erika said disbelievingly.

-Excuse me? The colonel's angry tone was back again and his face likewise reddened.

-I'm sorry colonel. I was thinking out loud. I didn't mean anything by it. Erika apologized. *Jesus! A quill?*

I thought they were just joking at my expense. This is what they use to write? Still? She was looking at the quill and ink recipient with a dishearten look. *It's gonna take me forever to do my calculations with this. I may as well have fallen in the Stone Age!*

-Miss Banner. Is everything all right? Do you need something else? The colonel was becoming anxious. He did not feel at ease with this strange woman. She dressed like a man and behaved rudely. She certainly didn't seem a lady.

-That blackboard would be nice and some chalk.

-I'm afraid that we are using the blackboard, *Dr.* Banner. Josh always made an inflexion whenever he pronounced the word "doctor".

-Well, okay then. If you won't lend it to me . . . She took the notebook, the quill, and the ink vessel and shrugged.—By the way . . . she said turning to leave.

–That won't work.

-What won't work? Josh asked confused. He hadn't determined yet whether he liked this woman or not. She certainly was attractive in a strange kind of way. She behaved like no other woman had behaved with him or any other men around. She certainly wasn't shy and she did not show fear when treating with them or respect for that matter. She wore pants that exposed her forms in a very indecent way, but she seemed not to realize that. And she seemed intelligent although a little crazy.

-Your cannon. It is a cannon model, isn't it? She said nodding toward the artifact on the table.

-Of course it will work. I designed it myself. Josh answered with a mixture of anger and amusement. *What did a woman know about war artifacts?* –I think you better worry about house chores and leave war and its artillery to men. Erika was flabbergasted. *What an asshole! Well, let him take his pride and shove it up his ass!* -Fine. Whatever you say . . . I would step aside if I were you when you first try it. Good day gentlemen. Erika said with satisfaction as she left. She was enraged. She definitely and positively could not live in a time like that. A time where men treated women as inferior beings and not as equals . . . *Please God! Let me find the way to go back to my time! Please, please. Let them be working to take me back. Let my team realize where I am and help them find the way.*

She went back to Anna's place and sat in a chair. Without wasting any more time, she started making calculations on the notebook. She had to scratch many pages and throw away a few. *Goddamn it!* It was a nightmare to write with that thing. Hadn't pencils been invented yet? –Anna . . . do you know what a pencil is? Erika asked without raising her head from her work.

-Of course. They use them in some schools and in stores. Do you need pencils? Maybe I can go to the general store and see if they carry them?

-Oh, would you? That would be so kind of you . . . I feel like I've been a pain in the ass to you . . . But I want you to know that I really appreciate you taking me under your roof. This time Erika raised her head to look at Anna who was looking back at her with gentle eyes.

-It's all right. At least I have someone to talk to, someone that is not judgmental and don't look down on me.

-Oh Anna. You are better than all the people in this fort. I bet you are!

-Thanks! I don't know about that, but it's nice of you to say so. I'll go now to the store. I need to pick up some things, anyway. She undid her apron and let Erika alone to continue her calculations.

Erika was concentrated in her work, when a sudden and strong knock at the door startled her. *Damn it! Who can it be now? Anna said she did not have visitors frequently.* –I'm coming. Erika said rising from the table. She went to the door and opened it. An enraged Josh was in front of her. He was all dirty with black smudges on his face and part of his body. Erika bit her lips. She was having a hard time trying not to laugh. Only the look in Josh's eyes kept her from doing it. –Josh.

-How did you know? He said in a low strained voice. She could tell he was trying to contain himself.

-Know what? She asked playing innocent.

-That the cannon wouldn't work properly. He answered between his teeth.

-Obvious reasons. The design is wrong for starters. She answered all smug.

-I know that. What I want to know is how do you know the design is wrong?

-I told you I'm a physicist and that's physics 101 or maybe 102, I can't recall. Physics of projectiles.

-I'm not even gonna try to ask you what's physics 101 or 102. I don't even wanna know. And I probably am crazy and I'm going to be the laughing stock of the whole fort, but do you know how to fix it?

-Of course! I told you it's easy.

-Would you help us? He said still speaking through his teeth. He was having a hard time trying to control his temper. Erika could tell.

-Humm. On one condition. Erika was enjoying this. *Where is your pride now, ha? You are at my door begging. Well at Anna's door. Wait, maybe I can get his help. Humm. If he was capable of designing that thing, maybe he can help me with my work to go back home. I have to approach this in a smart way. Negotiate. I need to negotiate with him, but . . . making him think that he is winning.* They were still at the door. Erika's hand rested on the door, holding it open.

-Well? Josh asked impatiently.

-Well what?

-What is your condition to help me improve my cannon?

-Ah, that. Lend me a blackboard and some chalk.

-Is that it? A blackboard?

-And your help in return.

-My help? In what matter?

-With my calculations and work. You seem an intelligent man enough and I need help to go back to my ti . . . home.

-Thanks for the vote of trust. He replied sarcastically. –So you need someone to take you safely home? To take care of you on the way?

-Not exactly. More like help to get me home but by adding brains into it. And someone that knows well the natural reserves around here. For example, whether there are mineral deposits and stuff like that.

-Okay, you lost me. I have not the slightest idea of what you're talking about. We need to have that pending conversation but I have not the time right now. Something has come out that I need to take care of. So, I'll be busy all day long but I'll come back later and we'll talk.

-Okay.

-So, will you help me then?

-Will you give me what I asked?

-Damn it woman! You're a pain in the . . .

-Ass, I know. But will you give me what I need?

-Yes. But I'm giving you two things for one. So, I'll also take one thing else for me. As he said this, he grabbed her by the waist with one hand and pushed her inside the house. He closed the door with the other hand and without giving Erika time to react he lowered his head and kissed her. Erika lifted her hands to push him, but he was a big man. He was at least four inches higher than her and he was too strong. At first, his kiss was more like an assault than a kiss. He was taking out his frustration on her. But as he felt the softness of her lips he softened the kiss and started an exploration of Erika's mouth teasing her with his tongue to open her lips. Erika had been caught by surprise and her first reaction had been to defend herself. But he was a good kisser. He seemed to know exactly what she liked in a kiss. So, she opened her mouth tentatively to see how he would go on. He introduced his tongue inside her mouth and began a soft battle with Erika's tongue, savoring all hidden spaces inside her mouth. She was surprised at how well he tasted, like sugar and salt and herbs. Erika slid her arms up his chest and felt his hard muscles. She wrapped them around his neck. When Josh felt her response he pulled her against him and deepened the kiss. One hand was behind her head holding her in place and one went down to her bottom, where he pushed it toward his hard bulge. *God! This man knew how to kiss! And he was touching her as any man of her time would have. Who would've guessed! Well, that surely is something that has not changed through time.* Abruptly, as suddenly as he had grabbed her he released her. Erika was disoriented for a moment when he let her go. Then, she slowly raised her head to look at Josh. He was breathing fast and with difficulty. –I'm sorry. He said with a low and husky voice.—I got carried away.

-I could see that. Her voice was also low and raspy.

-You didn't stop me precisely.

-I tried to, at first.

-But not later you didn't. He continued obstinately.

-Well, I also got carried away! It's not only a man's prerogative. Women can get carried away too. She answered back angrily. How could he do that? One minute he enraged her, the next he carried her to heaven and then he figuratively let her bang hard and sound.

-I grant you that. I've got to go. We'll talk later. I'll send for you to help me with that cannon. He frowned and turning around opened the door and left without giving her time to reply. *Damn this guy! First he kisses me. Then, he makes it seem like I throw myself at him. Typical man's behavior.*

Josh had stomped out of the house and almost knocked Anna down who was coming back from the store. He touched his hat as a sign of greeting and continued on his way. Anna entered the house and glanced at Erika with curiosity. –You have something on your cheek. A black spot. And she signaled the place to Erika. Erika was still recovering from the kiss. –I'll go wash my face. And she went into the bedroom.

-I got your pencils. Anna informed her from the kitchen. She was putting the things she had bought away in the cabinet.

-Thanks, Anna. I'll be right out.

Josh was angry. *Damn it! Damn that woman! I don't have time for this now. I need to concentrate on keeping us all alive in this fort. Those Indians are going to attack at any moment. But I just can't seem to keep her out of my head. She is so peculiar and strange. And she talks and behaves different to any woman I have known. She cusses a lot too. Not even the whores from the saloons speak like that. And those odd clothes! I have never seen pants like those she wears. Those seams don't look like man-made, they are too perfect, too equal, no woman or man sews like that. They seem like made with a machine, but there's no machine that could make that and if there is, I've sure as hell never seen it. They also have that metallic thing instead of buttons to hold them together. And the shoes, they are also unlike current men shoes, not to mention no self-respected woman would wear those. They are not Indian moccasins, 'cause Anna was wearing moccasins when we found her and those were completely different. And to top it up, she seems to know military artifacts thanks to that damn thing she calls physics. And she knows how to respond to a kiss. A hell of a kiss too, nothing shy about it. She is not prudish as most women are when a man kisses them for the first time. She did not try to hide the fact that she knows how to kiss. She's been kissed before and I don't mean a peck. But she is no whore either. She is too well educated. That I can tell. In a word, she is a puzzle and I have to find out where she is from and how she appeared so sudden. Because she appeared from thin air. I'm sure of that 'cause I had just passed through that place a minute ago in my reconnaissance and she wasn't there. Then when I turned, there she was. She will tell me but I have to make that damn cannon work properly first. And those requests she made, the blackboard! What in hell she needs a blackboard for? Is she planning to start a school? No. She said she needed my help to go back home. And she needs my help. Well, maybe on the way I'll get to know her more intimately. If that kiss was a prelude, I wonder how it would be to have her in my arms under my body. Damn it! Not again! I need to focus and stop behaving like an adolescent on his first date. Damn that woman! Damn you, Doctor Erika Banner! I'll get in your pants and then get you out of my head.*

Josh arrived at the colonel MacPherson's office.

–Miss Banner has agreed to help us review what went wrong with the new design. But she'll need the blackboard in order to write her calculations.

-Are you sure of that, Josh? After all she's only a woman. It's not her job . . .

-Yeah, I know that. And I don't understand it any more than you do, but somehow she seems to have the knowledge. I've been over the design over and over again and I can't find the problem. We need to have those cannons into operation as soon as we can, otherwise we are vulnerable to any attack and I am just not referring to the Sioux.

-All right Josh. So far you have been right with your recommendations. You would have made a fine soldier. It's a pity . . . The colonel sighed and pensively with a lost gaze he continued:—Let's give

Miss Banner a chance. Though I have to tell you son, that is an unusual woman.

-Yeah. Let's send her the blackboard. Jason agreed with a sullen look. He turned around and shouted:—Soldier, take this blackboard to Miss Banner. She's staying at Miss Anna's place. And ask her when does she think she can have the calculations ready. Tell her that it's urgent we finish this design as soon as possible.

-Yes, sir. The soldier answered and quickly calling for help he went about to carry out his orders.

Anna was preparing food, again. Erika was helping Anna washing the dishes from breakfast. She was thinking in the meantime that it was just incredible how much time you had to put into preparing meals during this time. You hardly had finished eating breakfast when you had to start working on lunch, then, no sooner you had finished lunch you had to start preparing dinner. It seemed that in this time you spent most of your time cooking, without taking into account that in between, with the little time left, you had to do household chores that she just took it for granted at home, like making the bed, washing the dishes, washing clothes. And what about sew your own clothes for God's sake? And the preparation of the meals, that was just so hard! You had to dry herbs, salt down meats to keep them fresh . . . And it seemed that you also had to stay all day long warming water for cooking and other things, for preparing tea and coffee. *Man! There is no time to rest around here! How do they do it? No wonder women don't study. How could they? When? And then, if they are lucky they will have to take care of a husband and children. Lucky my ass! If I had to live in this time I would stay celibate. Wait a minute! I am stuck in this time . . . No, I'm not. Yes, I am, unless that Neanderthal cowboy, who by the way kisses like a modern time guy, or better* –a small voice inside her head added—*helps me.*

-Erika? Are you all right? Anna asked her. –If you keep rubbing my basin like that you are going to take the enamel off. Erika stopped her hands and looked at Anna shocked.

-Oh! I'm sorry Anna. I . . . I got distracted thinking. I usually do, think I mean. That's what they pay me for, thinking, you know? Well that and other things. Erika finished with a forced smile.—I'll better go back to my calculations, that is if you don't need my help with something else.

-I don't think so. I want to keep the few things I own for now. Anna smiled mischievously.

-Oh? Erika looked with astonishment at Anna, and then saw she was smiling. –You're joking! And they both laughed. At that precise moment a knock sounded on the door. The soldiers were bringing the blackboard and chalk that Erika had requested. They put it against a wall and delivered the information Josh had asked them to.

-Soldier, you may tell Josh that I need to see his calculations and design in order to make the necessary corrections. Actually, I need him to tell me what exactly are the modifications he wants and what does he want to achieve. I'm not going to do his entire job for him or do everything all over again. Better yet, you tell him to come over and make himself useful. Erika told them with that commanding tone that her team knew so well but that here in this time was so unheard of coming from a single young woman. The soldiers were so astonished that all they could do was nod and respond:—Yes, ma'am. And as that, they left. Anna was holding back a laugh. She certainly hasn't seen before that the soldiers became speechless at a woman's command including a few that were old enough to be their father. Less than half an hour later a strong knock on the door startled them.

-Who is it? Anna asked.

-Josh, came the low voice.

-Josh, how nice of you to come so fast. Erika teased him, although his expression was murderous.

-Would you care to join us for lunch? We were about to. Anna intervened before Josh could respond to Erika's open mocking.

Josh sighed and turning around spoke softly to Anna, the way he always seemed to address her. Erika thought how odd it was that he always behaved with Anna as if she was about to break while with her he seemed to be on the verge of loosing his temper at all times.

-I . . . certainly Anna, if I'm not intruding. And perhaps afterwards, and now he turned again to face Erika,—we can discuss what you kindly requested of me through my men. He finished through his teeth, almost growling.

-Your men? Erika raised her eyebrow.

-While they are military, they respond to me for the time being as I'm working with the colonel. So, I would appreciate it that in the future if you have any other requests of that kind, ask them in a way that don't make me the laughing stock among them. Is that clear? Or . . .

-Or what? You're gonna spank me, big boy? Erika asked daringly. No sooner the words had escaped from her mouth, she regretted them. What was she thinking challenging him like that? She should be compliant so he helped her going back home. Nonetheless, she was behaving like a thirteen year old. *God! That jump in time must have affected me!*

Josh's eyes shone with a dangerous glint and he took a step toward her, but in that instant Anna's voice was heard.

-Lunch is served. Please sit down. Josh . . . Erika. They both stayed there facing each other like two enemies about to start a battle for a few seconds, until Anna cleared her throat and both snapped out of it. The three of them sat at the table then and ate in silence for a few minutes until Josh started to explain Erika what were his ideas about the modifications that he wanted to make on the cannons. After they have eaten, he showed her his calculations and the drawings for his designs.

-So basically what you want is that the cannons have a greater range, improved accuracy, and more power. Erika summarized after Josh explained what he had tried to do.—Then what you need to do is rifling them.

-Rifling? What is that?

-Well, you make spiral grooves inside the tube. This imparts a spin to the cannonball, which serves to gyroscopically stabilize the projectile improving its aerodynamic stability and accuracy. You could also change the shape of the cannon balls, you know, making them longer, not quite spherical but more like oval. Also, you could make the cannons so they are loaded by the breech instead of the muzzle.

-All right slow down, gyroscopically, aerodynamic? What is that?

-Ah, gyroscopically means that it works as a gyroscope, basically it is a device for measuring or maintaining orientation. You don't know it? When was it invented? I can't remember if it was invented in the early 1800s or the middle . . . Erika was walking around the room trying to remember while she mumbled to herself.

Josh was looking at her with a frown trying to understand all those new concepts and unknown words she was saying. —No, I don't know what a gyroscope is. But for what you're telling me, with the spiral grooves we can control better the orientation of the cannonballs?

-Yes, exactly. See, you have the knowledge; you just don't know the concepts. As for aerodynamics, it's just the study of the air and how it interacts with a moving object, namely the cannonballs in this case. Leonardo da Vinci wrote treatises on aerodynamics, Isaac Newton and others too.

-Who?

-Oh, never mind.

-So, can you do the calculations and the designs for the spiral grooves and the new shapes of the cannonballs and the other things you have told me?

-Sure, piece of cake. Just a series of equations and formulas. I need to know the length of the tube and the bore diameter, the weight of the cannonballs, their diameters, the material . . . Erika continued walking around the room while listing the data she needed, deeply involved in her thoughts. Abruptly, she turned around and realized that both Josh and Anna were looking at her with an expression of awe on their faces. She came to a halt and stopped talking.

-My God! Josh blurted out.—You really know all these things. I have never met anyone with so much knowledge, but for a woman . . . Who are you? Where do you come from? He was piercing her with his look as if trying to see inside her.

-I . . . Let me finish helping you with this and I'll tell you everything. Erika said, suddenly nervous about the oncoming explanations. What if he didn't believe her? What if he thought she was crazy? What if he refused to help her? –I prefer to concentrate on one thing at a time.

-Yeah, you're right. As much as I'm intrigued to know your story, this is something we need to have soon, the sooner the better. I'll make sure you have all the information you need and when you finish or if you want to ask me something, just send word with any of the soldiers. Now, if you'll excuse me ladies, I'm going to go.

Josh turned to leave when Anna called him and asked him something quietly. Erika was already engrossed on the work she had at hand so she didn't notice the quiet exchange.

Many hours later, Erika stood up from the chair and stretched. The lower part of her back ached as well as her shoulders and her legs were stiff. She had been sitting a long time to continue writing on the notebook the colonel had given to her since the blackboard was full with equations that she didn't want to erase. Anna had been cleaning the place, sewing, and preparing dinner. She had also gone out once but Erika had been so absorbed with what she had been doing that she hadn't noticed. She hadn't been aware either of a few soldiers that had brought something and taken it to the bedroom. Erika loved math and physics and projectiles design and operation were something she knew well. She enjoyed her work and any work involving problem solving. This had become a new task for her so she had immersed herself with enthusiasm as she always did when facing a new challenge. Now Erika looked at Anna, who was already setting the table and asked her in astonishment. –Oh, Anna, what time is it? I didn't realize it was so late. I should've helped you.

-You were so concentrated that I didn't want to bother you. Anna smiled but her smile was strained. –Let's have supper.

-Anna what's the matter? Erika could be a scientist and could get distracted with her work but she could also be very observant and she detected that something was wrong with Anna. She was edgy, not her usual gentle and nice.

-Nothing. Why do you ask?

-Anna, I haven't known you for long. In fact, we've only met a couple of days ago, but you seem tense to me. Please tell me what's bothering you. Have I done something to upset you? Am I too much of a burden to you? 'Cause I could . . .

-No, no Erika. You haven't done anything and I'm glad you are here. You keep me company, although you are certainly an unusual woman. She smiled at this.—It's just . . . that cannon you are helping Josh with . . . I . . . I'm afraid they're going to use it against Chetan and his people and I don't want anyone else to die. I don't want Chetan to die! I'm sure he will come to get me. Her eyes were brilliant with moist and she was wringing her hands.—You know, they are not like us, they cherish and respect their women. I'm the mother of his son and he won't rest until I'm back with him or die in the attempt.

-Oh, Anna. I had no idea. I didn't think . . . When I agreed to help Josh I didn't realize it was to fight against your husband's people. My God! I'll talk to him. I'm sure he'll understand.

-No, Erika. He won't listen to you. He doesn't know it's the Sioux he's fighting against. And even if he knows he won't mind. Indians are Indians to him, for him they're our enemies. Tears were rolling down her cheeks now.

-Oh, Anna I'm so sorry. Instead of helping you, I'm hurting you. Erika went to Anna and hugged her, trying to soothe her. –There must be something that we can do . . .

-There isn't. Chetan is going to die and if he dies, then I have nothing to live for. Anna got free from Erika's arms and run to her bedroom leaving Erika there in the room with a worried expression on her face.

CHAPTER V

Erika did not sleep well, though she should have. Later on last night, when she went to the bedroom, she found Anna slept in her bed. She had fallen asleep with her clothes on, clearly she had cried to sleep. Erika had found that instead the blankets on the floor, someone had brought hay and arranged it into a kind of bed. Someone too, probably Anna, had put some sheets and blankets on and added a pillow to make it more comfortable for her. Anna was a good person, Erika had thought, and she didn't deserve to suffer like she was suffering. Without thinking, Erika had probably contributed to make her a widow. *Shit! That woman has done nothing but to help me since I came here. She had been kind to me, and understanding and not judgmental. And how do I repay her but by getting her husband killed. Good for you! Jaee! There must be something I can do. I have to talk to Josh at least. I'll tell him that unless he promises me not to use the cannons against Anna's husband's people I won't give him the design. Then he won't help me getting back home. Shit! Damn it! Crap! Son of the b . . . So, am I willing to sacrifice my chance of getting back to help Anna? After all, I don't know her that well. And once I go back to my time I won't see her again. I won't even know what would become of her life here 'cause she isn't even an important personage. There will be no record left of her in history . . . No! I can't do that to her. She may not be a grand lady or someone that will change history but she is good and she has a son. And she is so young . . . I will talk to Josh. He must understand. And if he doesn't I can always find somebody else to help me, right? Right.*

Erika set the alarm of her wristwatch to go off early, before Ana wake up. She got up from a restless sleep and put on her blouse and jeans. She quietly left the bedroom and washed her face on the kitchen basin. Then without making any noise she left the house. It was dark outside. Dawn was close but it hadn't arrived yet. *Crap! I forgot to bring a light.* She started to walk being careful where she stepped until she halted abruptly. *Where does Josh sleep? I don't even know where he lives. I've just been to the colonel's office. I don't even know if anyone sleeps there. AHHHHHH! Why didn't I think of that before having this wonderful idea? How stupid can I be? Well, there is nothing that I can do now. I'll just have to wait at the office door until someone arrives and ask where Josh is.* When Erika arrived at the colonel's office, she looked in the windows but there were no lights on inside. She sighed and seating against the wall embraced herself for a long wait.

-Erika, Erika. Seems I'm always waking you up. Josh was shaking her gently. Erika opened her eyes and yawned.—I wonder if this is any indication of the future.

-What? Erika felt suddenly awake.—What did you just say?

-Well, I have woken you so many times by now that it is becoming a habit. But I'd rather waking you up in my bed, this is not very rewarding. Josh's voice was low and soft but a mischievous smile appeared in his mouth.

-What? Erika was taken aback for what he had said. The thing about the future had startled her.

-Never mind. What are you doing here so early? Have you finished the calculations? Why didn't you send for me?

-Okay, okay, slow down. Why you always have to fire a barrage of questions at me? I need to talk to you. But I need a coffee first. Erika said grumpily.

-Is it about the cannon? Should we take this conversation to a more private place? Josh asked getting serious now.—Come on, let's go to my quarters. He said when he saw Erika nodded.—Since you don't care about your reputation, why should I? He shrugged and turned around indicating her to follow him. They walked in silence to a small house near by. It was almost the same as Anna's, except that his had no second room to serve as bedroom and a small bed was placed against the farthest wall. –Come on in. He indicated to Erika opening the door.—I'll give you some coffee. I think I still have some left. He opened a small cabinet on the wall and took out a metal cup. He poured some coffee from a battered metal coffeepot that was on a small table and offered it to her. –It must be still warm but if you want I can heat more water and prepare fresh one. Erika took the cup and tried the coffee. It was not too warm but it was still drinkable.

-I'm sorry, I didn't offer you. Would you like some sugar or milk for that?

-No, thanks. It's fine as it is.

-All right, so shoot. What is it? Did you realize that you are not so smart after all and you couldn't improve the cannon? He took one of the chairs by the table and sat down stretching his long legs and crossing his arms over his chest. A smug expression was on his face and he adopted an indolent stance.

-You wish. Erika answered dismissively drinking the coffee. —The cannon design is ready and it will work smoothly, but I w . . .

-Great! He said interrupting her and almost jumping out of the chair. Let's make the modifications then. If you give me the new specifications I'll put some men to work on it immediately.

-NO! Erika shouted startling Josh.

-What do you mean "No"? He questioned angry. He stood up and approached her. He lowered his head frowning at her and grabbed her arm. —What kind of game are you playing? Do you have it ready or don't you?

-I do! She shouted again. She sighed and put the cup on the table. —Please answer a question first. She lowered her voice this time trying to calm down.

-What? He almost growled.

-Are you going to use those new cannons against the Native . . . the Indians? He was standing very close to Erika. His hand was still on Erika's arm but he wasn't squeezing it so tight now.

-Of course! What did you think? That we wanted them to collect them? Or to decorate the fort?

-Stop being so sarcastic! She shouted again and raised her head to look at him with a fierce expression. It was her turn to frown at him.

-Damn it! He growled again and lowered his head. His lips pressed hard against hers and with his free hand on her waist he pushed her toward him. Erika was so shocked that she didn't react at first. Then, she raised her hands up to Josh's arms and tried to push him. He had taken out his hand from her arm and was holding her head close to his. Erika was so enraged that she pushed with all her force. When Josh realized that Erika wasn't responding to him but pushing, he let go. He raised his head but still kept her close with his hands on her waist. –I'm sorry, I . . .

-Are you crazy? Erika shouted not letting him finish.

-*You* drive me crazy. He took his hands out of her waist and grabbed both her arms.—You are the most infuriating woman I have ever met. You make me act as a mad uncontrolled man. I have never treated a woman so rudely before. Believe me, I am not proud of how I react with you.

-Don't you throw this on me! I have made nothing to get your attention on this way.

-You kissed me back that one time.

-That doesn't mean you can attack me.

-You are right. I apologize. I was out of line. I don't have any excuse, except that you infuriated me so much that I just lost it.

-Well, learn to control better.

-I usually control myself just fine. He said between his teeth. He released her and passed his hand over his hair out of frustration. –Tell me what all those questions regarding the cannons were about. He said with an even voice now.

-It's just if you shoot those cannons to the Indians, you'll kill them.

-Well, that's the idea. Better them than us.

-But you don't understand . . . You'll kill Anna's husband and she is suffering and she . . .

-Wait a minute. What is Anna has to do with it? Anna is not married. Maybe those damn Indians raped her or abused her or maybe not, but she certainly couldn't regard them with feelings other than hatred or disgust.

-You are wrong. Anna is married to their chief and she wants to go back with them.

-You are not making any sense woman. How would Anna want to go back to them?

-Well, did you talk to her? Have you asked her?

-Of course not. We thought that it was indelicate and inappropriate to ask her such questions.

-So you simply assumed she was being kept captive by the tribe without even asking her if she was?

-Well yes, how can she possibly want to live with those savages . . . ? Josh was walking along the room now, passing one hand over his hair one and again disheveling it.

-Hadn't you noticed how sad she is? How she is making an effort not to break up in pieces?

-Yeah, but I thought she was sad because the things they did to her. That she was in the process of healing, of recovering from that experience . . .

-Well, you are wrong. She repeated firmly.

-And you say she wants to go back to the Indians? He asked incredulously.

-To that Sioux tribe, yes. Josh, why don't you go and ask her? She told him more gently this time. She sensed that all Josh had wanted all along was to protect Anna. That deeply inside he really thought she was grieving because something horrible had happened to her. And not even in his wildest dreams it occurred to him that Anna was worried about her Sioux husband.

-All right Erika, I'll go talk to her. He gave in with a sigh.

-What about the cannons? Erika asked anxiously. –Do you still plan to use them?

-Let's hear what Anna has to say and we'll see. He didn't compromise.

They both went towards Anna's place in silence. The day had already broken and the sun was starting to shine in the blue sky. When they arrived, Erika went in first letting Josh outside in case Anna was not presentable. –Anna, are you awake? Erika asked entering the house. Anna was already preparing breakfast.

-Erika! Anna turned around surprised. –Where were you? I was worried, I woke up and you weren't here. If you had to go to the outhouse you should've waited for me. You know is not safe for a woman alone at those hours of the day. Anna's eyes were swollen and red. It appeared that she had been crying some more this morning. And her face showed marks of worry.

-I'm sorry that you worried about me. I went looking for Josh. Erika explained, speaking gently.

-Josh?

-Yes, he's outside actually. He would like to talk to you. Can I ask him to come in?

-Of course, please do. Erika opened the door and summoned Josh inside. Josh got in and took out the hat that he had taken before leaving his house.

-Good morning, Anna. He greeted Anna gently but his jaw was set.

-Good morning, Josh. A smiled spread on Anna's face but she looked weary and strained. –Would you like some coffee? Always the good manners.

-Please. Josh sat down on a chair and placed his hat on the chair at his right.

-Erika, please sit down too. I'll serve breakfast and we can talk over it. Erika sat at Josh's left side leaving the fourth chair in front of him for Anna. She was tense waiting the outcome of this conversation. What if Josh asked Anna and she denied everything she had told her? What if Josh refused to not use the cannons? What she, Erika, should do then? Tear all her notes, burn them, so Josh could not use them?

-Anna . . . Josh was holding a cup of coffee on both hands and was looking at the coffee inside, suddenly nervous. –Erika has told me that you are concerned about those Indians being killed. I would like to know . . . Is that true? You don't want them to get hurt?

Anna stared at Erika for a long moment without saying anything. Then, she turned her gaze to Josh and sighed.

-Yes, that is true. I don't want you to kill them. They may be my . . . husband's tribe, the Sioux. I am married to the chief. Josh snapped his head and looked at Anna with wide eyes.

-And if it is them, would you like to go back to him? He asked cautiously now.

-Yes. Without hesitation.

-And why do you think they attacked us?

-Because you took me away from them.

-And when they come, do you think if you go back with them, they will stop the attack?

Before Anna could answer Erika asked. –Do you think they will come here? How can they find this place?

-It's not a question of if but when. They'll track us. They are excellent trackers. They'll follow our trace. Josh's face showed admiration. He admired them! How bizarre! To hate somebody but at the same time admire him. –Anna, would you be able to tell it's them? Are you sure they won't attack us if we let you go?

-I'm sure I'll recognize Chetan, my husband, even his horse if he is riding it. And if you let me go, he will order his people away. He just wants me back. But if you doubt me, when they come, I can go alone.

-No way in hell. I won't let you get out of this fort alone until I am completely sure they will not harm you. Josh said sternly.—Even though, how can I be sure he will go peacefully after you are with them? I have a responsibility to the people in this fort until more back up arrives. How can I trust he won't attack us afterward?

-Well . . . Erika stepped in.—You could have the cannons with my specifications ready to attack. Anna and I will go to the Sioux and talk to them and make sure they will go peacefully. But if they show signs of an imminent attack you can fire the cannons. Anna

took the hand that Erika was resting on the table.
They both smiled to one another.

-NO! Josh said firmly.—I won't risk the lives of two
women. What kind of man do you think I am? That
I let you two go unarmed and vulnerable toward
Indians? Have you lost your mind?

-Well, you could teach me how to shoot and with a
rifle or a gun and the cannons ready it would be safer.
And you could come with us too to speak with Anna's
husband. I'm sure he is more *civilized* than you give
him credit for. Erika finished sarcastically. But Josh
didn't catch her sarcasm; he was deeply in thought
assimilating what they had told him. He abruptly rose
from the table.

-I'll have to think about it. In the mean time, can
you give me the specifications of the cannons to start
right away?

-No, unless you promise me not to attack the Sioux.
Erika added stubbornly.

-I won't attack them before talking to you. You have
my word. But I need them ready as soon as possible
because right now the fort is vulnerable before any
attack from *anyone* since our cannons don't work. He
said gritting his teeth.

-Okay, if you give us your word. Here. Erika tore
out two pages from her notebook and gave them to
Josh.—Everything you need for the modifications is
in here. If you have questions, come and ask me.

-Thanks. I'll talk to you later. He picked up his hat,
turned and left. As soon as he closed the door, Anna
went to Erika.

-Do you think he'll honor his word? That he will not
harm the Sioux? Anna anxiously asked Erika.

-I think he will, but you know him better than I do. Erika replied. –He doesn't strike me as a bad person, you know?

-I may have known him longer but you sure know him deeper. Anna said wisely.—He has never spoken to me the way he speaks to you. This is the longest conversation we had since I arrived in here. You two seem to connect. Anna finished smiling.

-Don't be silly, Anna. It's just I have a strong character. He respects you whereas me . . . I don't know, I seem to bring out the worst in him.

-That's 'cause he likes you. Anna smiled again.

-No way! What is he, thirteen? Erika cynically asked.

-I think you make him nervous, 'cause you are so direct and upfront. Men are not used to women being strong, they like us to be soft and shy and accommodating.

-Well, I'm definitely not any of those things.

-Poor Josh. And they both burst out laughing.

CHAPTER VI

Josh didn't come back until the next morning. When he did, he looked tired. The three of them sat together at the table for breakfast again.—I've been thinking about what you said yesterday. He said after they had finished eating. –The two of you will go out to an encounter with the Sioux after you identify them, Anna. But you have to be real sure is the same tribe. I'll go with you and we all take weapons. The cannons will be ready to fire at the first attempt to attack on their part. If I see they try anything to harm any of you, I will shoot them. And believe me, I am a very good shooter. I'll take two or three before they get to me. I want to teach you to shoot right away, Erika. Anna, do you know how to shoot a rifle?

-Yes, but I am sure I will not need it against . . .

-Those are my terms. Unless you accept, I'll start firing those cannons and the army men will start shooting their rifles. We have to be fast. A sentry spotted some Indians this morning. They are trying to surround us. It's a good thing the fort is on an island, 'cause that'll force them to split and cross the river to have some men on the back of the fort. That should delay them for a while. The bad part is that we don't have anywhere to run if they are too many. With the basic modifications you designed, Erika, we can have some cannons ready for tomorrow. So, tomorrow at noon, we'll set a meeting with them. And with that he stood up from the table and asked Erika to go with him.

Josh took her to the back part of the fort where there was an area of open ground.

-Are you going to wear those pants tomorrow? Josh suddenly asked her startling her and getting her out of deep reflection.

-What?

-I asked if you are wearing those pants tomorrow for the meeting with the Indians. Josh repeated.

-Yes! Why? They are comfortable and I have no more clothes.

-Just checking. I sure would like to see you wearing a nice dress, but I reckon that for tomorrow they are more convenient. You'll be able to ride better on those.

-Wait. You said riding? As in horse riding?

-Yeah!

-Do you forget I don't know how to ride a horse? She asked in apprehension.

-You rode with me for five hours. I think that is as good a teaching lesson as any. Besides, I'll take your reins. Your only job will be to hold on and not fall from the horse. He was amused at her distress.

-Okay, she said giving in, though not without some anxiety.—Let's get started with the shooting lesson then.

-Right. First I want you to learn how to shoot a pistol. Then I'll teach you how to shoot a rifle. A pistol is better for close range while rifles are better for distances farther than 100 feet. However, the pistol will give you one shot only so you better be damn sure you aim well, 'cause you won't have a chance to shoot a second time. Here. I'll teach you how to use it. Jason showed the pistol to Erika, who was flabbergasted at the sight of it.

-This is a flintlock gun! How primitive! *Of course, we are in 1821. Colt hasn't invented his six-barreled revolver yet.*

-What do you mean, primitive? This is a state of the art pistol. Josh said offended.

-Never mind. Erika sighed. —Just show me how it works. I don't think I've ever seen one of these.

-All right. First, half-cock the hammer, like this. Then, pour a measure of gunpowder down the barrel. Just this much. Wrap the bullet in a piece of cloth like this and ram it down the barrel on top of the gunpowder. Next, place a small amount of gunpowder in the flintlock's pan. No more than that. It's only for the sparks. Snap the frizzen in place over the pan. The gun is now ready to shoot. Now, when we get to that meeting with the Sioux, your pistol will be charged already. You'll only have to fully cock the hammer, like this and pull the trigger if you need to fire. But I wanted you to know how to charge it, in case you have time to charge it and fire a second time. In the event that we need to use our weapons, that is. Now, hold it and feel it. Get comfortable with it. Erika did as told. The pistol was heavy, more than she had expected. She grabbed it in different ways, shifted it from hand to hand.

-Okay, I'm ready.

-Pull the trigger.

-Where do I aim?

-This first time, just shoot. I just want you to get used to the gun in your hand and how you feel it when you shoot it. We'll aim into a target later. Erika tried to shoot but the trigger was difficult to pull.

-Wow, it's so hard.

-Yes, here let me help you. Josh taught her how to hold the pistol with two hands. How to properly position her fingers and how to stand and breath adequately. Erika shot several times to catch the rhythm of it. When she started to feel comfortable with the pistol, Josh changed it for the rifle.

-Here, let's now try with the rifle. It's different than the pistol because is longer and heavier. But it works basically the same as the pistol.

-Wow! It's a Model 1803 US flintlock rifle by Harpers Ferry Armory.

-Good! You know it?

-Not really. I've seen it in muse . . . Never mind. Just tell me how to use it. Josh stared at her in wonder but he did not say anything, continuing with the lessons.

-Fine. To shoot the rifle you have to support it against your shoulder, like this. All right then . . . Josh helped her with the rifle too. He was patient and gentle. He corrected her position. He made sure she loaded both the pistol and the rifle precisely how it should be. And after all this, Josh instructed her how to aim.

–Well, now that you have the hold of it, let's really
see if you can shoot what you aim for. The first shot
was not very good, it was well away from the target.
Neither were the second nor the third. Erika was
both exhausted and hungry. And her mood was also
blackening.

-I'm sorry. I cannot seem to grasp it. It's just my hands
move when they shouldn't; they're sweaty and stiff. I
don't think I have it.

-Erika, if you don't know how to shoot well, and by well
I mean, you being able to reach any part of the body
when shooting, you won't accompany us tomorrow to
that meeting with the Indians. It's too dangerous and
I'm not about to risk your life without a minimum
of protection. So, breathe now how I taught you,
concentrate, use your knowledge, and shoot.

*Knowledge! Of course! Physics! Now I have it. I just have
to calculate the distance, the average speed of the bullet with
the time it takes to impact, its weight . . . Got it!* She turned
to Josh with a big smile on her face and told him. –I
think I got it now.

-Let's see then. Erika prepared herself, standing as
Josh had told her, breathing as he taught her and
shot.

-That was amazing! Josh exclaimed excited. –Do you
think you can do it again?

-I can try. She was so happy now, her smile was huge,
lighting up her features. She shot again.

-Excellent! Right on target.

Erika turned around to face Josh with a joyous
expression. He took her in his arms and lifted her,
whirling with her. Both were laughing. Abruptly, he
stopped and slowly and carefully put her down. He

looked at her intently and she gazed at him. He was giving her time to say no. She didn't say anything, just stayed there, watching him, waiting. Finally, he lowered his head and kissed her, gently at first, more deeply after a while. She put her arms around his neck. She had dropped the pistol when Josh had picked her up. Josh tightened his embrace. They were stuck together from knee to chest. He deepened his kiss introducing his tongue inside her mouth. Teasing her with it. One of his hands went to her breast rubbing her nipple through the blouse fabric. She could feel his erection protruding from his pants in her stomach. A warm feeling spread over her body and she lifted on her toes. Josh put his other hand on her buttocks to place her more comfortably toward him, so he positioned himself between her legs. He introduced his hand through the opening of her blouse loosening a button. He stopped suddenly and separating a little, he unbuttoned Erika's blouse. When he saw Erika's laced brassiere he was shocked.

-That is the tiniest corset I have ever seen in my entire life. His voice was hoarse and rough and his breathing was fast. Erika's eyes were closed, she was breathing hard too.

-That is 'cause is not a corset, it's a bra. She said without thinking.

-A bra? Josh gulped. —Is that new underwear for women? 'Cause last time I checked, not even the girls in the saloon wear things like this.

-It's . . . it's from my time, I mean where I come from. It's very common there. Erika wasn't thinking clearly. She was still distracted by Josh's kiss. Suddenly, she realized Josh had stopped kissing her. He was fascinated with what he was seeing. Erika became self-conscious and tried to cover herself with her blouse, but Josh put a hand over hers and said:

-Please, don't cover yourself. That is the sexiest thing I have ever seen on a woman. What about . . . ah . . . about underneath those pants? Are you wearing something remotely similar? His breathing had not reached a normal rhythm yet and he was having trouble to express coherently.

-Panties. Erika was getting uncomfortable now. After all, she was talking about underwear with a man from the XIX century. Certainly, that could not classify as a socially accepted conversation.

-Panties? What are those? May I see them? Josh was hovering over her like a wolf salivating before its next meal.

-Certainly not! We are in a public place. Someone may come by at any moment. Besides, I think this is getting too far. She buttoned her blouse and put a hand on his chest.

-No, you can do this to me! Look how you got me. Please Erika! A glimpse? We both know I'm going to see them shortly anyway.

-What? Wait. You think we are going to end up in bed?

-Sure, sooner or later, I'm going to have you under me. Josh answered confidently.

-What about my reputation?

-You left clear the first time I met you that you didn't care about that.

-That doesn't make me a whore!

-I never said that. I just said that I'm going to make love to you.

-Ah . . . ah . . . Erika was speechless. *The arrogant bastard!*

-Now, don't sidetrack me. Show me.

-Not in a million years! You bastard! And she stomped out of there.

-Oh, it won't be that long, believe me. And when it happens, I am going to enjoy all that temper of yours, sweetheart. He shouted watching her go. And he burst out laughing.

Erika arrived at Anna's place and slammed the front door. The noise startled Anna who was unfolding and smoothing out some clothes.

-Erika? What happened? Is everything all right? Has there been an attack?

-No, nothing like that. It's just that man infuriates me. She said between her teeth.—He is so . . . so . . . Oh, sometimes I would like to kill him. He makes me so mad. Oh! What is that you're holding? Those are beautiful! She inquired noticing the clothes that were in Anna's hands.

-Oh, do you like them? It's my clothes, my Sioux clothes. I'm gonna wear them tomorrow. When I go back to Chetan. She said smiling. Her eyes were brilliant and happiness showed all over her face.

-Anna . . . Are you sure is Chetan? I mean, what if they are a different tribe? Erika looked at her with concern.

-No, it's Chetan all right. I saw him. This morning after you left with Josh, I went to the sentry box and I told the sentry there that Josh had said it was all right, that I would probably know that tribe and he had asked me to identify them. So, he lent me his hand held telescope and I spotted them. They are all

there, all the warriors that accompany Chetan. I even
glimpsed Chetan himself. It's weird, you know, it was
as if he wanted me to know it's him, because when
Sioux hide you cannot see them so easily. Anyway, I
have to prepare myself. Oh, Erika, I'm so happy, I am
happier than I've been in weeks. I'm going to see my
son again, hold him, touch him, sing to him again.
And Chetan . . . I am going to be with him again, my
love . . .

-I'm really happy for you, Anna. I really hope that it's
him and you get to go back with him. I'm going to
miss you though.

-I'll miss you too, Erika. You have been like a sister to
me. Anna approached Erika and hugged her. Erika's
eyes were moist. In the short period of time they had
met, Erika had grown to love Anna as a dear friend.

–Erika, will you go with me tomorrow early in the
morning to the river like the other day? I want to
bathe before I meet Chetan again.

-Do you think that is a good idea, Anna? If Chetan
and his men are so close they could see us in the river
and they could come to get you. And if any of the
men sees them, they could start shooting. Wouldn't it
be safer for you to bathe in here?

-You are right Erika, I don't know what I'm thinking
anymore. I just want to leave, that's all.

-I know, honey. You will be with Chetan tomorrow
and we'll make sure you are so beautiful that when he
sees you he's going to know it's been worth to come
and get you. I'll help you. Oh, I wish I would have
some of my creams and perfumes to lend you.

They spent a large part of the afternoon carrying
buckets of water to fill the big metallic bathtub

Anna had. They even filled a big round wooden tub she owned too. By the time they finished bringing the water, they were so tired, they just prepared themselves a sandwich on a loaf of bread with some cold meat and cheese, accompanying it with a glass of milk that Anna had bought at the fort small store. Josh had made a quick visit in the evening to remind them to be ready by 11:30 a.m. the next day. He had taken a quick look at Erika and had smiled playfully, to which Erika had turned her back on him. Erika and Anna went to bed early that day, having agreed to get up early to make breakfast and then take the longed bath.

The next morning while Anna made breakfast and heated some of the water for their bath, Erika busied herself by making the beds, Anna's and hers, although if Anna left today, Erika would not need her bed anymore. Anna had told her the day before that she could keep everything in the house for she would not be taking anything with her except for her Sioux clothing. Now Erika swept the bedroom's floor and straightened up the bedroom, which was not very hard as Anna was very tidy and there weren't many things in the bedroom after all. She opened the window to let some air in and went to the main room to see how she could help Anna.

-Well, I'm ready with the bedroom Anna, what can I do to help you here?

-Not much, really. Breakfast is ready. I'm keeping it warm so we eat it after we take that bath. But you can finish filling the bathtub with cold water until it's lukewarm. If you insist on washing my hair though, you can put on some of my clothes, so yours remain dry. I figured that although you are taller than me you are so slim that my skirts will fit you.

-Okay, I will change, then. I'll be right back. Erika went through Anna's wardrobe and took out a blouse and a skirt and put them on, leaving her own clothes on the bed. She also took out two big towels, one for her and one for Anna and one smaller towel for Anna's hair. When she entered the room, Anna was already in the bathtub, washing herself with a sponge.

–Anna, are you going to shave your legs? 'Cause I haven't found a shaver . . .

-Shaving my legs! What a funny idea, Erika. I have never heard of that before. Do you shave your legs? I noticed when we were bathing in the river the other day you don't have any body hair on your legs and under your armpits either.

-Oh! Erika froze for one moment. *Fool! Another mistake! I definitely talk too much. That's right! Women didn't start shaving until the XX century.*—Never mind Anna. Forget what I just said. But to answer your question, where I come from, women do shave their legs and armpits. It's just a habit, really. She shrugged. –You have so little body hair though that you probably wouldn't need to shave much if you'd live where I live. Anyway, let's get your hair all clean and smooth. Do you have vinegar?

-Yes. Is it for the hair? We don't need it. Look, Erika! When I went to the store I bought this bottle of liquid soap for the hair. The clerk told me that it is new and it smells good. Women in the big cities are using it, so I bought it.

-Let me see that. Erika said looking at the bottle with suspicion. Anna gave her the bottle that she had conveniently left at one side of the bathtub. Erika opened the bottle and smelled it. She poured a small amount on her hand and inspected it. –Yes, as I suspected. It seems to be grinded soap with water and some herbs. Well, it's better than nothing, at least it smells good. But we'll use the vinegar too, because it will get your hair shiny and it won't smell bad, I promise. That one I know, my grandmother taught me. She poured a small amount of the *shampoo* on the superior part of Anna's hair, and also in the lower part, and start rubbing gently. When she finished, she rinsed her hair with some water pouring it with a big ladle. She left the water fall on the wooden floor, since Anna had told her that the water would run through the cracks on the floor. She had been right. *This place must be cold in winter.* Erika thought. When Erika saw there wasn't any soap left on Anna's hair, she mixed some vinegar with water in one of the basins and rinsed Anna's hair with this mixture, combing it at the same time until there weren't any tangles left. Erika wrapped Anna's hair in a towel.

-There, all ready.

-Thank you Erika. Anna said wrapping herself up in another towel.

-You're welcome. This was a wonderful girly time. I haven't had so much fun since I was little and played with my girl friends and our dolls. I'm going to take my bath now.

-Are you sure you're all right with that small tub? Anna said glancing doubtfully at the round wood tub.

-Yes, don't worry. I won't wash my hair today. I'll wash it tomorrow. Now hurry and get dressed. It's getting late and we still have to have breakfast before Josh comes to pick us up. When Anna came back into the room, Erika was drying herself.

-Wow! You look beautiful. Anna had her Sioux dress on and was wearing the moccasins. She had combed her hair in two braids at the way Indian women used. Her blond hair was brilliant and her face was radiant.

-Do you really like it? Anna asked anxiously. It's gonna be tough around here when people see me in my Sioux clothes. They won't like it.

-It's okay. Josh and I will be with you. If any person tells you anything . . . Erika replied with a fierce expression.

-You look nice in women clothes too, you know. Anna commented softly surprising Erika.

-You think so? Well, now that you're leaving, I may use yours since you don't want them. But for now I'll keep to my clothes. Josh recognized they are more convenient for riding. She finished with a gesture.—Let's eat.

CHAPTER VII

The three of them approached the group of Indian men that were waiting for them at the other side of the river. They were mounting the most beautiful horses Erika had ever seen. Two were covered with white and brown spots. One was all black with a light brown mane and one was all white. There was even one that looked like a giraffe with small brown speckles all over it. The men were all dressed in buckskin shirts with beads, beaded leggings and moccasins, and one had a feathered headdress. All of them were seated on the horses with a proud stance. Their bronze skin and their hawk like features gave them an appearance of classical beauty. Erika thought that on the whole this was the most handsome group of men she had looked at in her life. Their age should range between 25 and 35 years. Erika was dazzled with this group of pure breed Native Americans. She was also nervous and sad. Nervous because Josh, riding a horse at her side, was tense and stern. She sensed that he was ready to start shooting at the minimum signal. Sad because she could see Anna's excitement and she didn't want her to go. When they were at a distance at which they could speak, Josh made them halt. There were five men on the other side. They were only three; Josh had not let anybody else come with them. Now, they looked at each other. Josh had situated his horse in the middle slightly ahead of Anna's and Erika's and was running his eyes slowly and cautiously over the men in front of them. Erika was studying them too, one by one, with open interest. But Anna had eyes only for one man: the chief, the one with the feathered headdress riding the white horse.

-Chetan . . . She called softly and low.

-Are you all right? Have they harmed you? Chetan spoke directly to Anna in his language.

-I'm fine. They have treated me well. They thought you were holding me against my will. They rescued me. Anna responded in Sioux language.

-You are my wife. Your place is with me. You will come with us.

-Yes.

-Why did these two come with you?

-Josh wanted to make sure that all you wanted was to take me back. He wants to be certain that you are not going to attack the fort.

-I don't want war with them. I just came to look for you, but if they attack us, we will fight them back as a few days ago.

-I know that. They didn't nonetheless and they would have not listen to me if it weren't for Erika here. She is my friend.

-Your friend is a strange woman. However, she does not look at us with fear in her eyes.

-Yes, she is different, but she is good and has helped me a lot. She smiled. Suddenly her smile faded and she looked concerned.—Who died in the battle?

-Akecheta and Kangee. Enapay was wounded and I sent him home.

-Oh, my God! Akecheta had a wife and a child on the way. And Kangee, he was going to marry Anpaytoo. Her face showed her pain and sorrow. She really liked those men. They were fierce warriors but also caring and attentive.

-They knew they could die when I asked them to come for you. Chetan said without showing a drop of emotion, but Anna knew that he really cared for all the people in his tribe and he was hurting inside.—The tribe will care for Akecheta's wife and child. Anpaytoo will find another good man in time.

-Yes, I know. Anna sighed. –What about Enapay? Is he going to be all right?

-He will be.

Erika was fascinated witnessing this exchange, even though she couldn't understand a word. When she went back she would tell John to teach her his language. She found it phonetically captivating.

-Anna? Josh intervened now without taking his eyes from the men in front of them. –Everything all right?

-Yes. I am sorry Josh. It's just those men who died in the battle against your army? I knew them. They were good men. Anyway, Chetan says he will go and take all his people with him if I will go too.

-Can I trust him to honor his word?

-Of course you can! He is a man of honor, he is . . .

-Only take my woman. Chetan interrupted Anna, addressing Josh for the first time. Josh turned his head to stare in surprise at Chetan.

-You speak my language?

-Little. Anna show me.

-You will go then and stop the attack on us?

-Yes, we leave. No more fighting. We no want more war to white men.

-We, the men at Fort Crawford, that is the name of the fort, won't fight you either. But I can't promise other white men won't.

-We take care of our people. If other white men fight, we fight. If white men want peace, we keep peace.

-All right, then. Anna,—Josh called her,—are you sure you want to go with them?

-Yes! It was Anna's only answer.

-Leave the horse. You will ride with me. Chetan ordered Anna turning back to his language.

-All right. Let me say good-bye to Erika. Anna dismounted and went toward Erika. Erika dismounted too.

-Why you got off the horse Anna?

-I'm riding with Chetan. He doesn't care much for the white man's horses. She smiled. —I wanted to say good-bye to you. You have been like a sister to me, Erika. I love you. I will miss you. I hope you can get back home too.

-I love you too, Anna. I really would like for us to be able to see us again. Good-bye. Have a nice life. Take care of your son and give him a kiss on behalf of his aunt Erika. Her eyes welled up with tears. They both embraced for a few seconds. When they separated, Erika cleaned her tears away with the back of her hand and trembling smiled. –Anna . . .

-What? Anna stopped herself and turned around to face Erika one more time.

-Your Chetan is a very handsome man. I see why you love him so much. She whispered. Anna smiled at her and said good-bye to Josh.

-Thank you for being so nice to me.

-Any time ma'am. He touched the tip of his hat. Anna went toward Chetan, then. He bent down over his horse and with one arm lifted her on the horse, putting her in front of him. Josh did exactly the same. He went close to where Erika stood and reaching down to her put her on his horse.

-Good-bye, strange friend of Anna. Piece. Chetan said in English addressing Erika for the first time. Erika gaped amazed at him and said good-bye. Chetan nodded to Josh, who nodded back and turning his horse around he left with Anna, followed by his men. They all turned his horses in turn to follow his chief without having said anything. Josh took the other two horses' reins and went back to the fort with Erika. An expression of relief, disbelief, and skepticism was painted in his face. If he had talked to Anna in the first place none of this would have happened. No men would have died. No men would have been wounded. Instead, they all had rushed to assume that Anna wanted to escape from the Indians whilst the opposite was true. She had a child with that Indian and he had found out now just because Erika had mentioned it. Those Indians didn't want war; they just had wanted what they thought rightfully theirs, which in this case that would turn out to be a white woman was a revelation.

Anna sighed and rested her head against Chetan's chest. She was at last with him, he was holding her again with his strong arms. And she would be in no time with her son. She was happy, but she also felt a little sad for the men that had died because of her. She moved a little to try to be closer to her husband. He tightened his arms around her and held the reins with one hand when he felt her move. –We'll be home soon.

-Are there only five of you? Anna asked him quietly now. She could feel the familiar warming of her body as his hard body touched her with the movement of the horse. She needed to get the memory of his strong body covered with sweat and close to hers out of her head now. Though she needed him, she knew that there would be time to be alone later. So to get distracted, she started to speak with him.

-Yes. We were eight at first, but with Akecheta and Kangee dead, and Enapay wounded . . . He shrugged.

-They thought you were hundreds, maybe thousands. They even had cannons. I was so scared they would kill all of you, especially you. I was terrified thinking that you might get killed. Anna violently shuddered. Chetan smiled arrogantly.

-Well, white men are not very good at tracking. We laid some traps for them, made them think we were many more than we actually were. Chetan told her matter-of-factly.—That guy, Josh, he is very good for a white man. He was making it hard for me to trick him. He is a good opponent. I respect him.

-Good, for he is a good man and my friend Erika likes him.

-So, you were scared for me? Chetan asked now changing the subject.

-Of course I was. You are the father of my son. I don't want him to grow without a father.

-Is that all? He asked sounding anxious. Chetan anxious? He was as firm and dependable as a rock. Anna had never seen him hesitate before anything.

-No, that is not all. She spoke so low that Chetan had trouble making out her words. He tightened his arm around her waist so strongly that she couldn't breath well. He didn't speak, but his breathing became harder and his heartbeat accelerated.—I don't want to live without you. I love you, Chetan. She continued in a quiet voice. Chetan lowered his head and kissed her hair gently. He told her whispering in her ear.

-We are not far now. We'll talk when we get there, my love. Anna's body shivered at that brief and soft contact and she sank more against his body, feeling his heat and his hardness, which had become her strength along the past five years.

Erika was standing in the middle of the room. She looked around it. Empty! Anna had gone! She was all alone now. What would she do if she didn't find the way to go back to her own time? Was this gonna be her life? Maybe she should've gone with Anna. At least if she had no alternative but to stay here she would've had someone to talk to. What about Josh? A voice inside her head asked. Josh . . . Josh was clearly attracted to her and so was she for that matter. But where could that go? If she was leaving, there was no point in getting involved with him. If she wasn't . . . Well, she was not going to become her mistress, not in this time. That would result in her being ostracized. He wasn't interested in getting married, he had left that very clear. Even if he was, she wasn't either. She definitely was not wife material. What was left for her in this time, then? She put her hands over her face in desperation. *No! I need to get a hold of myself! I need to calm down and think. Think!* Her team would not desert her. *They're probably working right now to take me home and I'm here feeling sorry for myself. What I need to do is focus. Right! What information do I need? How can I help them? I better sit down and write it down.* Once she settled on a course of action, she felt much better. She wasn't going to give up. Not yet anyway. *Not much time has passed by yet.* She thought. *I still have time, although I'm running out of it. I probably have to go back to the place where Josh found me. So I need to involve him, definitely. Besides, he owes me. He promised to help me. Just 'cause his problem is gone doesn't mean he's gonna bail on me. Okay, I need to study the location, thoroughly, to find out what is so special about that place. What else? What else?* She was picking her brains to make hypothesis and theories that could help her return. As ideas pop out she scribbled them furiously on the notebook. She wrote everything that came to her mind. Then, carefully studying all her notes, she put them in a certain order. By the time she rose from the table she had a plan to follow. She smiled confident. She would succeed. She would return home. The hell with this time, she wasn't cut out for it. She was way too valuable in her time, where she belonged.

The sun had already set, she noticed now with amazement. She should eat something before going to bed, but she was too tired with the events of the day. Emotionally drained. Anna and Erika had created a bond in the short time they had shared this place. Anna was an outsider just like Erika. None of them had belonged in this place and that had made them unite. Granted, Anna had been able to solve her situation in a much more easily way, but still, they had been alike. When Anna had left Erika had felt as if someone had taken away the only salvation board she had to stay a float. The only thing left for her now was swimming. But she would swim tomorrow, she thought tired. She went to Anna's bed and collapsed on it.

Anna was seated beside Chetan; they were celebrating a gathering in memory of the two brave warriors that had died fighting to get her back. All the people of the tribe were there; they were forming a circle around a big bonfire. An elderly was chanting a very old song to help the souls of the dead be reunited with the Great Spirit in the other world. They had prepared a big meal to remember the courageous warriors and wish them a safe trip to the spirits world. The flames reflected on the solemn faces of all present. When the elderly finished his chant, everybody remained silent for a moment as a sign of respect for the deceased. After a while Chetan stood up and silently extended his hand to Anna. She took it and stood up walking with him toward their tipi. Before reaching it, Chetan turned to her and asked her:

-Do you wish to kiss Chaske good night?

-Isn't he in our tipi? Anna looked at him confused.

-Not tonight. He is at Hantaywee's tipi. Hantaywee was Chetan's mother. Her name meant faithful and she had lived up to her name. When her husband, Chetan's father, had died, she had remained faithful to him during all her life.

-Then, let me see him before we go to sleep. They both went toward Chetan's mother's tipi and entered. Chaske was already sleeping on his bison skins bed. They greeted Hantaywee and Anna went directly to Chaske. She softly and gently caressed his face and hair, her eyes filled with tears.

-I missed him so much. He looks so peaceful.

-That is because you are home now. Hantaywee said.

Anna looked at her mother in law and smiled. She had been tough with her at the beginning, but they had grown to love and respect each other. Anna continued stroking Chaske's head.—He is so beautiful.

-He looks like her mother. Chetan added with a husky voice.

-Go now. I'll take care of him tonight. You need some time alone. You'll have time tomorrow to be with your son. Now you need to be with your husband. Chetan's mother advised in a severe tone that Anna knew was full of fondness and care. Anna blushed at the implied mention of their mating. She had lived for five years with the tribe and still it was difficult for her to regard sex with the naturalness the Sioux treated it. Chetan went out and Anna followed him. They arrived to their tipi and Chetan opened the flap for Anna to get in. Inside the tipi they faced each other and looked intently at one another's faces. They both undid their braids and let their hair loose. Abruptly, Chetan took Anna in his arms and kissed her, the way she remembered, passionately as if he needed to get her inside his skin. Anna put her hands around his neck. She trembled, titillating. Chetan took out her dress and gently placed her on the thick blankets that served as bed. Without taking his eyes from her, he took out his shirt and leggings and proudly stood naked in front of her. She opened her arms and beckoned to him. He did not waste a second to get on top of her.

-I can't wait. I have been without you for too long. He warned her with an intense look and a guttural voice. For all answer she put her arms around him and pull him to her opening her legs to invite him in. With a deep breath, Chetan thrust into her all the way. He was shaking. −I love you so much. He whispered and then passionately made love to his wife.

Later, he was resting on the buffalo skins with her very close to him. She was half on top of him and he was stroking her hair. −I was so afraid that you didn't want me. He was saying. −At first, when you disappeared, I thought you had escaped. That you hated me so much, that you didn't even care for our son. I even thought that maybe you didn't love him because he was mine. Tears rolled down from Anna's eyes wetting Chetan's chest.

-How could you think that I would leave our son? You and him are the most important thing in my life.

-I know that now, but back then I didn't know what to think. You acted as if you loathed me. Only when we made love would you surrender to me.

-That's 'cause I didn't want you to know I loved you.
I didn't want to give you all that power over me. I
didn't know you loved me too.

-We have been fools. Haven't we? He smiled. –Let me
continue, now. Mother, who is a world wiser than I,
told me that you couldn't have escaped, that you loved
Chaske. That you would never leave him willingly.
And then, some of the kids told me they had seen
how white soldiers took you by force. Still I wasn't
convinced you did go against your will, so it took me
several days and a confrontation with mother to go
looking for you. He took a brief break to kiss her. He
didn't seem to have enough of her. He then kissed
the tip of her nose and continued:—I was gonna
go alone. I did not wish to risk the lives of my men
just because of my stupidity, but they made me see
that we all would do the same for any of the women
in the tribe. So, I formed a searching and rescuing
party and left. We tracked the white men army to
that camp, where we fought. But you weren't there.
I didn't want to loose any more men so we retreated
and waited. He gulped now. Anna was stroking one
of his flat nipples while giving him small kisses on
the chest.—They guided us to that place, the fort. I
didn't know for sure if you were there, but the next
day, we saw you and your strange friend at the river.
Anna lifted an eyebrow. –When we realized you were
going to bathe we discretely moved away. I swear
we did not peek. I wanted to, peek at you I mean,
but you weren't alone. Anyway, after that, I made
myself and one of the men visible to their sentry, so
they would know we were there and somehow you
would hear it. Days passed however, and nothing

happened. I started to believe that maybe you didn't
want to come back to me after all. That even though
you had loved our child, now that you were among
your people, you had realized that was your place.
So, I talked to my men to decide what was the best
course of action and we decided to wait three more
days before retreating. I was desperate, I didn't want
to loose you, but I had to think about my people.
That night was one of the hardest nights I have ever
undergone. He turned now to rest full on his back
and put an arm over his face. Anna felt cold at being
deprived from his heat so she climbed on top of him
and rested her face on his chest. His heartbeat sped
up and she felt how he was getting hard. He went
on with his story. It was important for him that Anna
knew.—You were so near, but I couldn't grasp you. I
stayed all night long looking at the stars praying that
you decided to come with me, even if it were only to
be with our son. I made a promise, not to touch you
anymore unless you wanted me too. I was ready to
give you your freedom from me as long as you stayed
with the tribe. And then, the next day, the most odd
thing happened. A white flag was hoisted. And not
long afterwards, three horses left the fort. You were
on one of those horses. I didn't know what to make
of that. Were you coming to tell me to go away? Why
else would you be approaching with two other armed
people? Then I saw one of them was a woman. By the
way, I have never seen a white woman wearing pants
before.
-Yes, Anna smiled now. —Erika is unique.
-Anyhow, as you approached my heart raced. Maybe
that would be the last time I would see you, so I tried to

absorb you with my eyes, imprint you in my memory. But then, you said my name . . . You said it in a way that raised all my hopes. I don't recall exactly what happened next. My memory is blurred. Next thing I realized you were riding with me. And then you told me you love me. Chetan stopped talking, he was trembling again. He was overwhelmed with emotion. It was Anna's turn to talk.

-I knew you would come after me. I knew it because I know you. You are proud and brave and loyal. And you were not going to let someone or something take away what's yours. And I also knew, that no matter what, you would do anything in your power to recover the mother of your child. But I didn't know you loved me. I didn't expect it. All I hoped was for you to take me back, in spite that you probably would have another wife by then. I thought I could endure anything as long as I was near you and our son.

-I would never do that. I would never take a second wife. I want to spend all my time with you alone. The rest of my life if possibly. And I want more children. I want another son and a girl that looks like you, with your light hair and your fair skin.

-I'll give you all the children I can. We may have made one tonight.

-Let's make sure and try one more time. Chetan said turning Anna so she was trapped under him and kissing her again. He made love to her long and leisurely this time.

CHAPTER VIII

-Damn it, damn it, damn it! How did Anna do it? Erika shouted in the verge of tears. –How stupid for letting the fire died last night. Now I can't even light it to heat up some water and make coffee. How am I supposed to prepare food? I already ate the cheese and the bread that was left. She kicked the fireplace out of frustration and a cloud of black dust raised, blinding her. She kicked again and this time she hit the wall. –Ouch! Son of the b . . .

-Erika? Are you all right? The door opened violently and Josh was instantly by her side.

-NO, I'M NOT ALL RIGHT! She screamed at him. She was covered all over in black ashes. Her hair was disheveled and her dress dirty. She was wearing one of Anna's dresses 'cause her jeans wouldn't take one more day. She had put her clothes apart to wash them after having some coffee. The dress was a little short but it fitted her.

Josh roared with laughter and Erika just lost it. She jumped at him and started to pound him on the chest with her hands in a fist. –Don't you laugh at me! She screamed. Tears were now uncontrollably rolling down her cheeks, leaving white traces in her smudged face. Josh put his arms around her and pulled her toward him so her hands were squeezed between their bodies. She sobbed on her chest for a while. When Josh sensed she was calming herself, he separated her a little.

-Now, now. He took her chin and lifted it so he could look in her eyes. He stroked her hair with his other hand. –Tell me what is the matter. He asked gently.

-The matter is I feel so lost here. I mean, I'm a PhD, right? So I should be able to do these basic things, like to light a fire. She explained while cleaning out her tears with her hands, which resulted in more smudges on her face. Josh was intently looking at her trying to stay serious with great difficulty. With her face so smudged, she looked adorable, he thought.—But I have tried for hours and the fire never catches up, it always goes out. She continued. –I haven't been able to heat water to make coffee. And I really need coffee. She finished with a choked sob.

Josh sighed. –All right, first let's get you clean, you look like you had been working in a mine. Then, I'll teach you how to light a fire and we can prepare some coffee. He went to the basin and dampened a handkerchief that he took out of his pocket. He went to Erika and cleaned her face as if she was just a kid. She stayed still letting him do. –By the way, you look good in a dress. Are you wearing that same underwear from the other day? He asked now with a deepened voice.

-I don't think how that is any of your business. She replied with a frown moving away from him. He smirked.

-That's more like it. You are back. I wondered where the brave Erika had gone. She smiled ruefully. She realized he was just trying to get her back to normal.

-I was pitiful before, wasn't I? I'm sorry about my outburst. It's just . . . I miss Anna and her peacefulness. And . . . I haven't seen you in a couple of days. I thought you had left or something. With her gone . . . you are the only person I know here. Besides, you said you would help me and then you disappeared! She glared at him.

After Anna had gone with the Sioux, they had gone back to the fort and he had walked her to Anna's house. He had left without saying when he would be back. When he didn't show up the next day, she had started to panic thinking that maybe he weren't going to fulfill his promise. That she would have to do the things for herself. And then this morning at realizing the fire was out and she couldn't light it back, all the tension accumulated from her situation had made her lost it.

-I'm sorry. I've been busy preparing things for our departure. I haven't forgotten I promised to help you. In fact I came over to ask you when do you want to leave. Though I reckon we haven't talked about how it's exactly you want me to help you . . .

-Yeah, well we can do that chat now if you have the time. I'd really like to leave as soon as possible, tomorrow if we can actually . . .

-That soon, ha? I thought that maybe you would want to stay a few more days. It's summer after all and we

have five more months before winter. I figure I can
take you wherever it is you're going in that time. He
sounded suddenly nervous, unsure. He took his hat
and put it on the table. Then, he passed his hand
over his hair.

-Five months! No way! I need to go back home earlier
than that, otherwise . . . *I may not be able to get there
at all.* She thought in dismay regarding him with
astonishment.—And why would you think I'd stay
here more than necessary?

-To know each other. Because there's something
between us. He aggressively blurted out.

-Josh . . . She carefully addressed him.—I don't think
it is a good idea for us to know each other better,
I . . .

-Why? You're not married, are you? You don't wear a
ring. Do you have someone waiting for you at home?
He continued, stubborn.

-I'm single and currently without any relationships,
but . . . Josh, you don't understand, we can't. When
I explain you my circumstances, and I really, really
hope you don't think I'm crazy, you'll see why there
can't be anything between us. Josh studied her for a
few seconds, squinting his eyes. He opened his mouth
to say something, then seemed to change his mind
and instead replied:

-Let's have that coffee and we'll talk. I'm really
intrigued now.

   Josh taught her how to put the pieces of firewood
in the more appropriate way to catch fire. And then,
how to blow air so the flames would raise and slowly
burn into ember. *At least I know how to poke it.* Erika
thought watching Josh carefully in case she had to

do it by herself. She took some water from one of the buckets and filled a pot giving it to Josh, who put it in a hook on top of the hearth. –While the water heats, why don't you eat something? Josh asked Erika.

-I don't have anything to eat. I mean, there are some vegetables and grains but they need cooking and as the fire was out . . . Josh slowly stood up from the hearth and turned to look at her with something in his eyes that resembled rage.

-When was the last time you ate? He said in a low voice trying to control his temper.

-Yesterday morning I ate some carrots and I had some nuts for dinner.

-Carrots and nuts? My God, no wonder you are so thin! At first I thought it was the dress that made you look so skinny, but now I know better. Why in hell you didn't send for me or went to the colonel's office? You know the way. He sounded exasperated.

-I was busy doing some thinking and calculations and by the time I realized I was hungry and I didn't have anything left to eat, it was very late at night. She said defensively. She was getting angry. She didn't like to justify before others.

-That didn't stop you before! He growled.

-That was important! She yelled.

-And eating isn't? He shouted back. –Jesus, Erika . . . He tousled his hair once more by passing his hand through it exasperated.—I think the water is ready. He said calmer now. –Can you prepare the coffee or should I do it? He raised his eyebrows.

-I'll do it. Erika answered offended. Why they always had to end up arguing? Why he always got mad at her and vice-versa? She entertained herself in the preparation of the coffee while he scowled at her. Brusquely he left, coming back minutes later with a package wrapped in a piece of brown paper. Erika was at the table drinking her second cup of coffee. When she saw Josh entered the house she raised from the table and without a word she poured some coffee in a cup for him. Josh placed the package on the table and opened it. It contained some cured meat, cheese, and a piece of rye bread.

-Eat! Just that word. No apology for treating her so rudely or for leaving so brusquely without telling her where he was going.

-I'm not hungry thanks! She told him haughty. A vein jumped in his temple. He set his jaw, but didn't utter another word. Leisurely, he turned to watch Erika, who was seated holding her cup of coffee with one hand and looking at him with a daring expression on her face. Very slowly, he took the cup out of her hand and grabbing her arm lifted her from the chair. Erika was mesmerized by the look on his eyes. They were gleaming with something dangerous. She didn't see it coming so distracted as she was. Like a lightning his hard mouth was on hers. He intended to punish her but her reaction to the kiss disconcerted him. He had anticipated a furious response or mild acceptance but not this passion. Erika was holding him with her arms around his neck, hungry for his kisses. She had pulled closer to him and had lifted herself on her toes to reach him better. For just a moment Josh froze at this unexpected reaction. It didn't last much. He tightened his embrace and deepened his kiss. He put a hand on her buttocks and pressed her harder toward his erection. She moaned and he growled.

The kiss continued until both were out of breath. He raised his head to take some air and asked:—What about that thing about not getting involved? His voice was deep and guttural.

-To hell with it. Erika fiercely answered and attracted his head against hers. She was tired of being cautious. Okay, so what if this was only temporary? She had a handsome and willing guy at her disposal. She liked him a lot and he liked her in return. She wasn't sure she could go back to her own time. She was alone, scared, and frustrated at this possible outcome. So, right now she needed to distract herself of all that and what better way? Josh started to unbutton her dress. Actually, he was very proficient at it. Erika thought. He took it down and exhaled a long breath.

-You're wearing it! He whispered. His eyes were heavy-lidded.

-What? Erika was for her part so diverted trying to take out his shirt that she didn't pay attention.

-Your tiny corset, no, you called it differently, bra! That's what you said its name was. He admired it and then, put a hand over one of her breasts and gently rubbed her nipple. He kissed her again, tracing a path of little kisses over her face. Reaching her earlobe, he stopped there for a while. Absentmindedly he asked:

-How do you take it out? I wanna see you.

-In the back. She answered impatient.—There's a fastener. Unhook it. He returned to her mouth and, at the same time, put his hands around her and using his fingers he unhooked the bra. Erika started to take it out but Josh stopped her.

-Let me do it. His voice was low and rough. He bent, passing an arm beneath her legs and carried her to the bedroom, where he deposited her gently on the bed. She was disheveled, the dress half way on her body, her bra still on but loose. Her lips were reddened and swollen, and her eyes heavy-lidded, but he thought that he had never seen a more beautiful woman in his entire life. He placed one knee on the bed and bent to finish taking the dress off. He gulped.

–Wow! So that is a panty. I reckon I like it more than the current women's underwear. He studied it for a moment, then slipped it off. He took off his boots and stripped his pants and underwear off. He placed himself on top of her and continued kissing her. Erika had also watched him. He was striking, she thought. His broad shoulders narrowed into his hips. His body was muscular and lean. His chest was covered with a diamond shape of black hair, which continued in a line until reaching his pubis. But what was more impressive was his erection. *Wow you!* She thought. And she opened her arms to welcome him. He kissed her deeply, teasing with his tongue, whilst probing. And he caressed her all over. His hands touching and feeling her body, knowing her. She touched him too, the strong muscles of his arms and back, his well built pectorals, and his flat stomach. He opened her legs and entered her with one long slow thrust. She sighed at the feeling of fullness. She had made love several times before. She had had her share of failed relationships, for that matter, but never felt like this. She embraced him with her legs and offered herself completely to him. His thrusts became faster and stronger as he felt her enveloping him. She was so excited he was driving her crazy. She clung at him trembling. *Oh, God! Please don't stop!* She thought.

Ah! She climaxed so strongly she felt limp. Not soon afterwards he emitted a guttural sound and collapsed over her. He was breathing heavily. –God! That was . . . He couldn't finish. He had to take a deep breath.—I'll move in a minute.

-No! Stay. She protested.

-I'll crush you.

-Just for a while.

-Mmm. He nodded sleepily. After some time passed, Josh kissed her gently on the neck and moved to the side. He put an arm over her waist and pulled her toward him. –Let me recover for a while, honey. They slept for some time. Erika woke to Josh's caresses. –Why do you have those marks on your body, similar to the shape of the underwear you wear? He asked curious when he saw Erika opened her eyes and smiled at him.

-What? These ones? She pointed out her breasts.

-Yeah! Why are you fairer there than in other parts of your body? He was lazily drawing patterns on Erika's skin at the borderline of the two shades. He had never seen those marks in a woman before.

-That's because of the swimming suit. She trembled when he caught a sensible spot. She saw his surprised expression and she elaborated. –Where I live, we like to take sunbaths to get suntanned. And we wear swimming suits, mine is a bikini, a two-piece suit, like my underwear here. Other women wear a one-piece swimming suit.

He lifted his eyebrows. –In public? Where is that place where decent women go out almost naked?

-Not where, when.

-What do you mean? He was entertained with a freckle on her waist, slowly tracing circles around it.

-I come from the future. She blurted out. –From the year 2010.

He froze. His hand stopped on her waist. He didn't move, didn't talk. He seemed to be holding his breath, weighing up what she had just told him. Deciding if it was true or a very creative invention.

Erika let a deep breath escape. –I know how it sounds. I'm not crazy or making fun of you. He sat on the bed and studied her.

-You know? I'm here trying to make sense of a woman to whom I just made love. And I can't seem to come up with a reasonable and logic explanation. Why in hell would you tell me something like that? Number one, you think I'm stupid and you think it's funny to tease me. Naw! You know better by now. Number two, you're telling the truth. The problem is that truth is insane. Not, impossible! No one can travel in time. You just have your time, you are born, you live, you die. It's as simple as that! Nonetheless, there are certain things about you, odd things, your way of speaking and behaving for example, different from every person I have met along my life. The fact that you basically don't know how to do the simplest things, like the fire issue. So, the way I see it I have two options. Either I run like hell from you, and I'm not too fond of that –He scratched his head and made a gesture—because I'd sure like to make love to you again. Or . . . I believe you and start throwing away all my beliefs.

Erika was observing him flabbergasted. Was she wrong about him! Instead of calling her nuts or leaving, he was calmly rationalizing what she confessed.

-While the first is easier than the second, I'm inclined towards the second option. He concluded. —There's a catch, though. He touched the tip of her nose.—You'll have to prove it to me. Baby, you are drooling. He got closer to her and covered her mouth with his.

She knew! At that precise moment, she knew. She had fallen in love with that man. How had that happened? She had no idea. One moment, he annoyed her, the next she respected him. That revelation moved her foundations. What was she supposed to do now? Tell him? Stay with him? Leave? Life could be so complicated, and then more. He saw her struggle. He was that insightful.

-Whatever it is you are thrashing out, it'll have to wait, because now I'm going to make love to you one more time. I'll deal with your fixated ideas later. This time he took his time, driving her crazy yet again.

Several hours later, Erika woke up to coffee aroma. She took a sheet from the bed and wrapped herself up with it. Approaching the other room she saw Josh completely naked fixing some sandwiches with the cured meat and cheese. She stood there in the doorframe watching him move around the small kitchen, looking for plates and cups. His black hair was disheveled and he had beard stubble. Erika thought that he was one of the handsomest men she had ever seen. Actually, she'd only met another man that handsome, John, her co-worker on the NASA team. How odd, they resembled one another somehow. That's why she thought Josh looked familiar. He seemed to notice her and smiled.—You're awake. Great! I was getting hungry and you must be too. He served coffee on two cups and put them on a plate. Balancing it in one hand and the other two plates with the sandwiches on the other, he beckoned her to follow him to the bedroom. –We're eating in bed. I am not ready yet to let you go. I want to hold you some more. He put the dishes on a bedside table and sat on the bed, his back to the headboard. He then gestured her to approach and taking the sheet from her, placed her on his lap. –There you go. Now we can eat and you can tell me. He gave her a sandwich and a cup of coffee and started to eat his sandwich.

Erika told him everything. She told him when and where she was born. She told him about her parents, her whole family. She also talked about her growing up, the school, her friends, college, and the job she was currently doing. She talked about her time and the things in it. Josh listened to her mostly quietly, pensive, interrupting her sometimes to ask her to clarify certain things.

-Wow! You know Erika, that sounds so unbelievable that has to be truth, otherwise you have a great imagination. But to come out with those things, it's too much; no one could fabricate such amount of stuff by himself. Now show me proof, I need to see some proof. So I'll know I haven't gone mad.

Erika got up from the bed and went in search of her jeans. –You saw my clothes and shoes.

-I admit they're different to everything I've seen, but it doesn't prove anything. It could be a new fashion or from a different country. Maybe Europe. Josh shrugged.

-Look at this. This is a zipper. Zippers have not been invented yet. Erika said triumphantly showing him how the zipper worked closing from down to top and opening in the opposite direction.

-Interesting . . . but what I told you still applies. Josh entertained himself opening and closing it several times before putting the jean aside.

-Okay. Erika turned around the room looking for something. —I wish I had my calculator with me. That surely would prove it to you, but I lost it when I traveled in time. I know! My wristwatch.

-Clocks already exist.

-None like this one. Wait and see. Erika went to the wardrobe and rummaged through some clothes. —Here it is. I bet you will never see a watch like this in your whole life. She approached smugly to the bed, where Josh continued seated, smiling at her. She jumped on top of him and gave the watch to him. Josh took it and observed it thoroughly. Then, raised his head. —All right, so instead of a chain it has a wristband. Big deal! Someone may have devised it.

-No, not that, the features! Erika pointed out annoyed. —Look, it not only indicates the time but the date, and it's waterproof. If I sink it in the basin, it'll still work. Besides it has an alarm. Listen. She took it from him and put the alarm at exactly one minute after the present hour. After the minute passed the alarm sounded with a high-pitched tone. —It has also a light and the hands and markers can be seen in the dark.—Watch! And she put her hands around the watch to enact darkness. Erika showed him all the features the wristwatch had.

-Will it always work?

-I'm afraid it won't. It will stop when the batteries run down. Before Josh could ask, she explained.

–Batteries are what give the watch power to work instead of the spring. See, I'll show you. She went for a knife and opened the back cover to show Josh the small metal circle inserted on it.—Yeah, you don't have to remember wind it up but if you don't change the battery the watch will die. Josh gave her a grave glance.

-Well. Let's say I believe you. He gave in. –Tell me more about your world while I prepare us supper. He got up from the bed taking her with him. He kissed her with a slow deep kiss. –I still haven't had enough of you but we need to be fed. Put something on in case someone comes looking for me. He advised while he put on his pants without any underwear.

-I forgot about the others. Erika was stunned. Time had passed and she hadn't missed a thing 'cause she had been with him. –Don't you need to be somewhere else?

-I told the colonel I'd be here helping you preparing our departure. If he needs something he will send for me. But I don't believe he will now that the Indians had gone.

-I'll help you cut the vegetables. Erika said walking to the kitchen after him. She had put Josh's shirt on, to which Josh had dedicated an appreciative gaze. –So, what do you want to know? Erika sat at the table with a knife, some vegetables and a bowl.

-Tell me about all those things you use at home and at work that "make your life easier". That's how you put it, isn't it? He was busy arranging things for a stew.

-Well, for example we have electrical or gas kitchens. You just have to turn a knob and they will ignite producing the fire, which you can control, higher or lower. We have running water, you open a faucet and there you have it, hot or cold. We have dishwashers to do the dishes, washers to wash your clothes, dryers to dry them too. We have microwave ovens to heat water and food, food that is frozen and ready to eat after heated. We have refrigerators and freezers to preserve food and to keep drinks nice and cold. What I wouldn't give now for a cold beer. She sighed. Josh listened thoughtfully to all that while making their meal.

-It really sounds fun, your world. What's a microwave oven? He questioned puzzled.

-It's like an oven but instead of working with heat produced by electricity or gas, or fire, it works with very small waves, which bounce on the food making the molecules inside the food to move and release kinetic energy that works like fire to heat or cook it. Seeing Josh's confused expression she added.—It's an oven really that works faster than a conventional one.

-Electricity? He lifted his eyebrows.

-Electricity is what we use to provide illumination and power to run things and machines. For example, instead of oil lamps and candles, we use light bulbs that we turn on at a switch on the wall. Electricity is so wonderful! I really miss it. Televisions and radios work on electricity. And computers too! And we have all kinds of devices to listen to music and also phones and cameras and video cameras. Erika continued animatedly.

-Wow, wow, wow! Wait a minute. You're talking about things that I can't even picture in my head. Televisions, radios, phones, computers . . . What the hell is all that? You're driving me crazy.

-And there's more. She smiled. –Automobiles and airplanes and submarines and rockets. We've even traveled to the moon!

-Travel to the moon? You mean that moon that rises on the sky at night? She nodded smiling. –Men have gone there? How?

-In rockets.

-Man! I'd sure like to know your world. It seems so different from this life.

-It is. I'd really like for you to see it, Josh.

-Now, slow down and tell me about all those things you mentioned. They finished preparing the stew and Erika told him all the details of the things we give for granted in our everyday life. She told him in simple terms that Josh could understand, not because he wasn't smart enough but because those things were inconceivable on those days for people who weren't in the scientific world. She spoke about how you can communicate nowadays using the Internet with people that is thousands of miles away, in other countries, even in different continents. How you can travel from one country to another in a matter of hours instead of weeks or months. All the things that are being continually discovered thanks to the new technology. Josh absorbed all that knowledge during the course of a few hours, inquisitive, making intelligent questions, doing his own educated guesses. He was astounded and impressed. The hours passed, Erika talking, Josh listening attentively. Day became night. They talked and they made love. Every time it was better than the previous one. Finally, just before dawn they fell asleep embracing each other.

-Wake up sleepy head. Josh was gently shaking her.

-What? She asked confused.

-Come on. Wake up.

-Already? How long did we sleep? Three hours, four? She yawned.

-Two. But you can sleep later. Let's freshen up. I'm all sweaty and sticky. And you too, you still have some ashes left. Besides, I want to get there before people start to wake up.

-All right, all right. Erika grumbled getting up. –But you have to let me sleep later.

-So, we are cranky in the mornings, ha? Josh smiled in amusement.

-When I have slept for only two hours. She put on one of Anna's skirt and blouse, without any underwear.

-You're not wearing anything underneath? His eyes darkened and his lids half-closed.

-I have to wash my underwear. I wash it everyday 'cause what women wear nowadays is too heavy and difficult to put on. She took her panties and brassiere, as well as her blouse, her jeans and Anna's dress and made a bundle. –I'll take the opportunity to wash them.

Josh picked up some soap and two wooden buckets and led the way. Surprisingly, he took her to the same spot where Anna had taken her that first time.

-This is the place where Anna and I came to take a bath!

-I showed it to her. He smiled mischievously remembering. –I saw you.

-You saw us when we came to bathe? She half-closed her eyes in suspicion.

-I only watched you. I couldn't take my eyes of you. But as I realized you were with Anna and she was going to take a bath too, I left. Hey! Don't look at me like that! I was going to bathe too. I like the cold water. Come on. Come with me. I'll scrub your back. I brought a brush. He grinned again with that playful smile of him.

She took the dress off and got in the water. It was as cold as she remembered and she shivered. Josh went toward her and hugged her. Then, he rubbed her skin to help her get warm. He washed her hair and her body scrubbing her gently with the brush. He then washed himself quickly and efficiently. Erika watched him in a daze, embracing herself to offset the cold a little. He approached her and kissed her, placing their bodies together. He adjusted her so she had his already erected organ against the notch between her legs. A heat spread through Erika's body and she forgot about the cold. Erika started to move her hips and taking Josh's hard penis, introduced it inside her. Josh sucked in air as he felt himself enveloped by her. He lifted her legs positioning her in a more comfortable way and thrust hard and deep. Erika almost climaxed, she was so excited. Josh could not hold it long and almost simultaneously they came.

Josh was panting, his heartbeat going fast. –We better get dressed and go back. The people of the fort must be already up. Besides, you have to tell me where we are going and what you want to do.

He helped her to get out of the water. They dried with the towels they had brought and put on their clothes. Erika washed her clothes with Josh's help, who was turning out to be a great aid with household chores. When they reached Anna's house, Josh asked Erika to prepare some coffee while he went to get some food for breakfast. They had run out of the things Josh had brought the day before. He also wanted to supply themselves with enough food for the road. By the time he was back, Erika had hung out her clothes to dry on a side of the room, had made some coffee, and was changing the bed clothing.

-Well. Let's have breakfast and tell me about your plans.

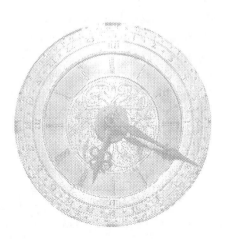

CHAPTER IX

-So, here we are. This is the place where I found you the first time. Josh was serious and stern. The day before, after he had made all the arrangements for their departure, he had made love to her intensely and passionately as if he knew they didn't have much time. He didn't like the idea of Erika going back to the future. He wanted her to stay with him. They had argued about it, nonetheless he had fulfilled his promise and had taken her back to the place where she had appeared. They had taken two horses, but she had ridden with him. Both wanted to stay as close as they could for the time they would have left. He now offered her a hand to dismount. It had taken them four hours instead of five because they had ridden at full gallop. Josh tied the two horses up to a tree while Erika was looking around at the ground.

-Look Josh, my calculator! She took what was left of her calculator, a bunch of broken pieces of plastic and electronic circuitry. –See, I told you I had it with me when I traveled through time.

-Mhm, he grumbled, still in a bad mood.

She was walking around in circles deep in thought. Josh had told her there were not mines or anything similar but plants and trees nearby. Nothing that would create an electric or magnetic field. As far as the sight reached there was nothing but prairies. Erika was mentally looking for ways to aid her team get her forward to her own time. She knew they were working on it, or at least she hoped they were. Unexpectedly, something called to her attention. A reflection not far from her. Josh and Erika seemed to notice it at the same time. Both approached the spot where something was sparkling. Josh got there first and ducked to pick up something.

-What is it? Erika came closer to him to peek at what was in his hand. He was examining it intently turning it around.

-It's a sort of mirror. He said in wonder.

-Let me see. Erika extended her hand toward Josh. –It's the front cover of a powder box! She said in amazement, laughing. –Josh! You know what this mean? She was excited with the finding, while Josh was frowning. He wasn't so thrilled about it. –This comes from my time. This means my team is trying to get me back. They're experimenting. Oh! I knew it! I knew it! She shouted excited.

-What next? He growled.

-There must be something else about here, the other part of the powder box. We look for it or we wait for another thing to come. She was already searching the premises.

-I think I found it. Josh said reluctantly. His aspect was grim. –Here. He gave her a round plastic cover. Attached to it there was a plastic wrap and inside it, it was a piece of folded paper. It read: *Bringing u back. Be one day after delivery –July 19. Or plus two days –July 21. Or plus three days –July 24. 12:00 m. Not fourth time. Teleporteam.*

-What does it say? Erika wordlessly handed over the powder box cover. She was having mixed feelings. She was glad she could return to her time, her world. But she didn't want to leave Josh. She loved him so much. Why did she have to find him here? Now? It wasn't fair. She had to renounce to one of the two: Her life of achievements, where she could be useful to mankind or the man she profoundly loved. Josh pulled her out of her abstraction. –What does it mean? And what is Teleporteam?

-Teleporteam is the name we auto-designated ourselves. Teleportation Team –TeleporTeam. She answered absentmindedly.—And it means that I only have one more chance tomorrow to go forward in time to my life. She raised her head to look at him. She hadn't wanted to, because she knew what she would find in his eyes. They were full of pain and anguish and love for her. He hadn't said anything to her. He didn't have to. She knew, she knew because of the way he had made love to her, how he had held her afterwards, fiercely as if he didn't want to ever let her go. And she also knew that her decision would hurt him, more than he would recognize. How much time had passed since she arrived? A week? Eight days. So little! And she had fell desperately in love with him in such short time. And she would lose him too in so a short time. She fought the tears that threaten to come out. Josh couldn't realize how much this hurt her too or he wouldn't let her go and she had to. She had to!

-I'm going to set a camp for us as we are spending the night. Josh told her matter-of-factly, but his face showed the strain. She could see he was barely controlling himself. He went to where the horses were tied up and started dismounting the things he had brought. Erika stayed on the same spot, her eyes closed, reining in her misery.

Josh lighted up a fire and put a pot with water in it to make coffee. –I'm going to see if I can catch something to eat. He grabbed a trap he had also brought and penetrated into a small forest west of their position. Erika slowly walked toward the camp and sat with her knees up and her arms around them. A haze seemed to have positioned on her head. She was numb. She was suffering but she couldn't find any other alternative. What was killing her, however was the fact that she was aware of Josh's silent suffering. She didn't want to hurt him, causing him this distress and nonetheless there was no other course. He couldn't go with her. She couldn't stay. Some time later, Josh came back with a rabbit. Erika did not know how much time had elapsed. Without a word, Josh took the pot off the fire and refilled it with water. Erika had let the water boil and evaporate. He took out a hunting knife and busied himself with the cleaning of the rabbit. He cut the rabbit to pieces. Then, he found a stick and pierced the rabbit's pieces with it. Finally, he set the stick over the fire on top of two rocks so the meat could cook up. Next, after washing his hands, he turned toward Erika and easily lifted her from the floor.

-Since we only have what's left of the day and tonight, I'm going to seize it to the max. And he rudely covered her mouth with his. Josh ripped away her blouse, buttons leaping all over. Erika didn't mind. She wanted him as desperately as he wanted her. He made love to her passionately and crudely and she responded with the same intensity, aware that this was really the last time for them. Afterwards, wrapped in a blanket they ate the rabbit, which was a little overcooked but good, and drank coffee. –What if you get pregnant?

-I won't.

-How do you know it?

-Because, she sighed,—I'm on birth control.

-Birth control?

-Yeah, it's something women of my time use to avoid unwanted pregnancies. Josh lifted his eyebrows.—You know I wasn't a virgin when we made love for the first time. I had other lovers.

-So what? So have I. I don't care. I care that you are with me now and I get to make love to you all that I want; that is until tomorrow. He finished with a grimace.

-Thank you. That's very . . . evolved from you. Though in my time we are more open to the sex subject, there are still some guys around that prefer exclusivity where women is related.

-That doesn't answer my question. Why would you be on the so-called birth control? You told me you weren't involved with anyone.

-I'm not. I wasn't. Not for a year, anyway. She went on.—There is this injection that lasts for three months and out of habit I continued to use it.

-I see. So there's no chance you would carry my child, then.

-Not much, anyway.

-That's a relief, then.

-Is it?

-Yeah. If it would be the slightest possibility you could get pregnant with my child, no way in hell I would let you go. He said bluntly and with that he turned her toward him and fell asleep on the blanket. Hours later, he woke her up. He was already hard and trying to enter her. Erika loved him sleepily and afterwards he held her closely to him. —Stay with me. He whispered.—We can have a family.

-Josh, please. She put a hand on his mouth to keep him from saying anything else. He took it and kissed it, kissing every finger.

-I love you. He said with a strangled voice, low and coarse.

Tears started rolling Erika's face. —I love you. She released her hand and put it on his face. —You don't know how much. But I have to go. I have to. I know you don't understand. I can't either. I don't know why this happened to us. Why we fell in love, when it is clearly impossible. But something tells me I have to go back to my time; it's like a hunch, more than that, like a sixth sense. Something that pulls me away from you . . .

He gently kissed her tears away. —I know what you mean. I sense it too. Like this is not our moment, that we are not supposed to have found each other now. But, damn it! I don't wanna lose you. I have never felt like this before.

-Me neither. She agreed. This time she kissed him softly and he loved her tenderly and slowly.

-It's time Erika. It's close to noon. He extended his hand to catch hers and pulled her to him. He bent his head and kissed her for the last time. A deep long kiss.

-I want you to have my wristwatch. Erika handed it to him. Her eyes were watery. She couldn't help it.—It will stop working eventually but I want you to have it.

Josh swallowed hard, sucking in air. —Okay. He nodded and took the watch. Erika went to the spot where she had found her calculator and Josh had told her he had found her. Josh stepped back away from her, watching her. —I love you. Suddenly, a white light appeared as if it was inside her, extending it outwards. It was so bright Josh had to shade his eyes. Erika mouthed an "I love you". The light extended until it covered her body completely, then abruptly it receded until forming a dot and then, disappeared, taking Erika with it. Josh fell on his knees. —Erika! Erika! He shouted.

CHAPTER X

-Erika! Erika! Someone was calling her. Someone was softly slapping her. Everything was black. The voices came to her muffled as in water. –Wake up, sweetheart. Come on, baby. Come back to me. She slowly opened her eyes, blinking several times.
-Josh? She whispered uncertain. A mouth was on hers, kissing her deeply. There was something familiar about this kiss and something different too.

Erika's team watched in astonishment at John kissing Erika. Had they had something going on? Luke glanced at Joy, who shrugged. Then both looked at Mark, who made a "what the hell" expression and lifted his hands in ignorance. John picked up Erika from the floor, where she had dropped the minute she had appeared in the teleportation chamber.—Let's take her to a hospital. The story is she fainted, probably from stress. He was already walking with her on his arms. The other three nodded in agreement.

-Ah, John? We can use my minivan. It's bigger and more comfortable. Mark offered.

-Okay, lead the way. John was striding while he carried Erika as if she was as light as a feather. Mark passed him and made his way towards the parking lot. Luke and Joy followed behind whispering to each other.

-Did she say John? Joy asked quietly to Luke.

-I think she said Josh. Luke whispered back.

-You sure? I think I heard John.

-No, I'm positive. She said Josh. I've a very good ear.

-So do I. John intervened now.—Come on guys, focus here. We need to get her to a hospital, quick. Both Luke and Joy hurried to catch John and Mark. In order to access the parking lot they had to exit the building and go through the security gate by the guards. The labs were in the second floor, so they needed to take the elevator to get to the ground level. When they arrived at the guard post in ground level, the guard looked at them with a surprised gaze.

-Wow! What happened to Dr. Banner? Is she all right? He asked concerned.

-She fainted. It's probably stress. John volunteered.

-We're taking her to a hospital. Just to make sure she is all right. Luke intervened.

-That's weird. The guard replied scratching the back of his head. –I didn't see Dr. Banner getting in this morning and I haven't left my post.

-That's 'cause she's been here all week. I think she's slept in the lab. Now was Joy's turn to speak.

-Yeah, we're under a lot of pressure. Jim, if someone asks we're taking Dr. Banner to the hospital and we don't know when we'll be back. Mark half shouted at the guard as they hurried through the exit doors

and went towards the personnel's parking lot. There
he led them to his car. Luke helped John to arrange
Erika as comfortable as they could in the back seat.
John seated with her and put her head on his lap.
Mark took the driver's seat with Joy by his side on
the co-driver's seat. Luke went to one of the seats in
the middle after helping John. Mark started the car
and left the parking lot driving efficiently but fast.
–Which hospital?
-To El Camino. John ordered.

Mark nodded and drove the car through the
streets web. –I'm going to take the 85 South. He
informed.

-You're driving. John answered absently. He was worried
about Erika. She hadn't regained consciousness,
although she looked like she was sleeping.

-What about traffic? Joy spoke through her hands;
she was nervously biting her nails.

-I don't think there's gonna be much traffic at this
hour, but if you have any suggestions . . . Mark was
concentrating on the driving but he averted his eyes
from the road to look at Joy. Joy continued picking at
her nails, denying with her head.

-Don't worry, we're almost there. It's not far. Luke
the eternal optimist intervened. –Anyway, if the GPS
indicated the way . . . Did you turn on the GPS?

-Ah, just did. Mark was embarrassed. He had forgotten
about the GPS with all the rush. He was worried about
Erika too. –The GPS shows we're five minutes away.

They arrived at the hospital in ten minutes total.
But all of them felt as if hours had elapsed. Mark
parked the car and all of them got out. John lifted
Erika in his arms again. None of the others dared say

anything to him or tried to help him. A nurse came immediately to him as they crossed the doors.

-What happened? The nurse inquired.

-She fainted. John informed her.

-I'll get a gurney. She walked away and in seconds was coming back with a gurney. —I already paged the doctor. He'll be here in no time. Please put her on the gurney. John did as told and backed away a few steps where the other three were standing in the hallway. The nurse was efficiently taking her vital signs. A man in his early forties wearing a white coat and with a stethoscope hanging from his neck appeared through a door in the corridor.

-What happened? He asked to no one in general.

-She fainted. The four of them repeated all together.

—She'd been subjected to a lot of stress. John added.

-How are her signs? The doctor now addressed the nurse while he checked her eyes with a pin light and then her pulse.

-Normal blood pressure, a hundred and twenty over eighty. Body temperature fine, 98F. The doctor nodded to the nurse and turned back to face the four people waiting anxiously there.

-Her vitals seem fine. All is normal, blood pressure, temperature, pulse . . . Her pupils reacted normally to the light. I don't see anything wrong with her except for maybe fatigue signals. I would like to admit her to observe her and run some more tests to make sure nothing is wrong. Are you her relatives?

-We're her co-workers. We work at the NASA's Ames Research Center. She's been working a lot lately . . . John stopped then. What could he say? We have been conducting teleporting experiments and it seemed that she teleported herself to an unspecified location and time? He looked at the others for help, but they were as perplexed as he was.

-I see. Does she have any family you can call?

-Her parents live in another city. She has a brother and a sister, but they also live far. We are the closest she has here.

-I'm afraid if you are not related to her I'll have to ask you to leave. There's nothing you can do right now, really.

-But, doctor . . .

-You can't . . .

-Leave?

Mark, Luke, and Joy started to speak at the same time. Fine, it's true they only worked together but they had been sharing a lab for two years now, endless hours of working. They had shared foods and jokes and pressure. They had suffered through good and bad times together in the project and all the strain it entailed. How could the doctor now asked them to leave? Didn't he know they were all worried sick for her? Couldn't he tell? The doctor raised his hands as if to calm them down. He opened his mouth to say something but at that precise moment John spoke.

-She's my fiancé. We're going to get married. At this everybody shut up. The doctor turned to watch intently at John. He seemed to be measuring him. He saw his serious stance and he sensed an iron will and determination.

-Very well then. You can stay. The doctor agreed.

-I'll call you guys as soon as I have new information. I promise. The doctor is right. There's nothing that you can do here right now. Go back to the lab. Finish recording all the data to have it ready for Erika when she recovers. If by the end of the day there are no changes, I'll call each one of you to your cell phones. The three of them knew better than to contradict John. After all he was second in command. Or at least that was the way everyone seemed to regard him. They said good-bye to him and left.

-I want to run a CT scan and some blood tests. The doctor informed John. John nodded. Hey, what the hell? He wasn't a MD. He was a PhD in math, a very smart man but he was no doctor. So anything to find out if there was something wrong with Erika. John thought. —Very well, we'll need her personal information to admit her. You can go to the admission desk. You know her personal information, right mister . . . ? The doctor raised an eyebrow.

-Dr. John McMahon. And yes, I know all her personal information. He replied sternly. The doctor acknowledged that and left with Erika and the nurse, while John went to the admission desk.

   Approximately four hours later, John was seating by a chair next to the bed where Erika was sleeping in a hospital room. He had the TV on but muted and he was blindingly staring at it. The doctor came in and John rose from his chair.

-How is she? Did you find anything? He asked him anxiously.

-The CT scan showed nothing wrong. The blood tests are all normal. She is as healthy as a horse. This is probably stress related as you said yourself. She looks extremely fatigued and strained. So her body is doing what she needs more, sleeping. So, I'd say she is going to sleep all night long. We would like to keep her until morning just to make sure. John exhaled a deep breath that he didn't know he had been holding.—You don't need to stay the whole night. The nurses will call you if anything presents . . .

-I'll stay. John interrupted stubbornly.

-Very well, as you wish. I'll come by tomorrow morning to see how she's doing. The doctor informed him and left afterwards.

Erika woke up disoriented. The sunrays were filtering through a blind. *Where am I? What happened? I thought I saw Josh. He was kissing me. Wait, that wasn't Josh. That was . . . No, I must be confused.* She looked around the room and saw John asleep on the hospital armchair. He was sprawled across the chair, his legs extended, his arms on each side of the armchair and his head resting on the back of the chair. His black hair was tousled and his face showed budding stubble. His clothes were wrinkled. However, he still looked handsome. He was one of the handsomest men she had ever seen and he reminded her of Josh somehow. *Josh!* Erika recalled everything now. She had left him. She had to. Sadness enveloped her. She was never going to see him again. John opened his eyes as if she had called to him.

-Hey! You're awake. He smiled. –How do you feel?

-A little disoriented but fine.

-Good. You scared the hell out of the guys and me. We thought you would never come back. Are you hungry? Do you want me to call the nurses?

-Some fried eggs and pancakes would be nice. She smiled back at him.

-I don't know about eggs but I'll ask. I'll be right back. He rose from the chair, stretched for a moment and straightened his clothes. Then, he left the room. Erika sat on the bed and slowly turned her head from side to side to check for any pains. No pain, just sleep as if she had been exerting herself. Some minutes later John walked back with a nurse. She smiled at Erika and started to take her blood pressure.

-I already paged the doctor. He will be here soon. But you look fine to me. I think he may discharge you today. She smiled through her explanation and efficiently smoothed the bed sheets and checked the water content in a plastic pitcher. After making sure everything was fine she was gone leaving John and Erika alone. John was standing in the middle of the room watching her with an odd expression. She was getting nervous by his intent gaze, so she asked:—What happened? I don't remember much, except for the intense light and then the lab.

-You appeared in the chamber and as you stepped out of it, you fainted. Then, you regained consciousness but fainted once more, so we brought you here. He told her succinctly. The doctor came in as Erika was about to say something.

-Hello Miss Banner, I'm Dr. Miller. Yesterday you were brought here because you fainted. We ran a series of blood tests and a CT scan and all of them showed nothing wrong. Dr. McMahon said that you have been under a lot of pressure from your work, so I think that you probably suffered a fatigue collapse caused by all the strain you have been submitted to. So, basically I'm going to discharge you today, but you have to rest for several days. I suggest at least a week.

-What day is today? How much time have I been sleeping?

-Today is Tuesday. You have been sleeping for approximately nineteen hours.

-Tuesday? Then I have to go to work! Erika opened the bed sheets and tried to get out of bed. –There's so much work to do, we need to . . . Wow! Erika stopped when she felt a little dizzy.

-Easy there. Both the doctor and John approached her, but John arrived first and put an arm around her shoulders protectively. –You'll feel a little dizzy because you have been sleeping a great amount of time. That's why you should take it easy and rest for a few days. You don't need to stay in bed, you can get up, but you shouldn't strain yourself. Perhaps Dr. McMahon could help you? You know, since you're getting . . .

-Sure, I can help her. I'll do everything for her. Her meals, whatever she needs. John interrupted the doctor. –Don't worry honey, the guys are collecting all the data, so we can analyze it. That'll take them a couple of days. We can take a few days off so you get well rested.

-Okay. Erika agreed reluctantly. –But a week is too much. Can't it be today and tomorrow? She didn't shake John's arm because she needed the support but that close contact with him seemed too intimate. They had always been friends, right from the beginning, they had joked together and laughed. But John was behaving different with her now, more possessive as if they shared closeness. As if they were romantically involved. And the way he looked at her, so intense, so purposefully. Maybe she was just tired from the ordeal she had gone through. Maybe she was imagining things.

-Let's do this. Dr. Miller took her chart and wrote some instructions on it.—You go home, rest today and tomorrow, and Thursday morning, around 9:00 am Dr. McMahon brings you for a quick check. If you are not tired and I find you well, you can go to work. How's that sound?

-Great! Erika tried to sound excited.

-All right then, while they finish the discharge paperwork, I'm going to the lab to fetch my car and some of your clothes. Erika lifted her eyebrows in a silent question. —I asked Joy yesterday to go to your place and get some clean clothes. They are at the lab. I'll bring them. You'll be all right, won't you? John watched her closely. —I'll be gone half an hour tops.

-I'll be fine. I think I'll take a shower in the meantime. Can I? She addressed the doctor, who finished writing on her chart and put it back at the bed's foot.

-Sure, just don't make any abrupt movements to avoid dizziness.

-I'll come back soon. John bent over Erika and brushed her lips. Erika was surprised but she didn't say anything. John turned around quickly and left. Erika stayed there motionless watching John go with a wondering look in her eyes.

-Well, here we are. How do you feel? Are you tired? Do you want to lie down? John asked solicitous. He left a duffel bag on the floor against a wall and closed the door. Erika turned to face him.

-John, really. I'm fine. She started to sound like a broken record, even to herself. —You needn't bother . . .

-You heard what the doctor said. You need to be taken care of and since I happen to be available . . . He shrugged. –That's what friends are for. We are friends, aren't we?

-Yes, we are. So, I wonder . . . why would you tell Dr. Miller you are my fiancé?

-Oh, that.

-Yes, that!

-It was the first thing that occurred to me. They weren't allowing any of us to stay with you. One of us needed to stay to check on you. You know, in case something unusual happened. After all, we don't know the effects of what you went through could have. John finished matter-of-factly. That was John, always attached to the facts, always cool, always under control. Except that there was something else John was not telling her, Erika could sense it, but she couldn't quite grasp it.

-And we continue as always.

-Until you say otherwise.

-John . . . I'm not kidding. I'm not one of your bimbos.

-I know Erika. Believe me, I know.

-As long as we are clear . . .

-Yes, I promise not to lay a hand on you unless you ask me to.

-John, I . . . I'm in love with someone else. Erika stated in a strangled voice.

-Josh. John pronounced the name in a whisper, as if in pain.

-How do you know? Erika's eyes opened wide in astonishment and sorrow showed in them.

-You said his name, twice. I figured that much. So, do you want breakfast or brunch? John changed the subject and went to the kitchen rolling up his sleeves. He had changed clothes and was wearing a sports shirt and jeans. Erika went to the living room and sat on the sofa.

-I'm so hungry that I could eat a cow, so whatever you have in mind is fine. She turned on the TV and started switching channels with the remote control without really watching.

-Okay, you just relax and I'll fix you something tasty. John was moving pans and pots and taking things out of the refrigerator and shelves. Some time later, John went to the living room and found Erika sound asleep on the sofa. He stayed there for a while just looking at her. She had huddled up and cried. He could still see the moisture on her face. He gritted his teeth and closed his hands into fists. A vein protruded on his temple. He took a deep breath and gained control over him. Then, bending over Erika, called her softly. Erika opened her eyes sleepily and smiled sadly.

-John . . .

-The food is ready. I decided that given the time we better have lunch.

-Okay. Erika rose slowly from the sofa and walked to the kitchen, where John had set everything on the table. –John, you shouldn't have bothered. John had prepared baked salmon with vegetables and rice; there was also a salad to accompany it. John shrugged and helped her to sit.

-It's better to cook for two.

They ate in silence. Erika was too melancholic to say anything. She was numb and too wrapped up in her unhappiness. John surreptitiously cast a glance toward her every now and then but didn't utter a word. Though Erika had expressed earlier that she was very hungry, she didn't eat much. She played with her food engrossed in her thoughts. John finished his meal and asked her if she was done. At her nodding he cleared the table while she remained seated with an absent gaze.

-I brought some movies. Do you want to watch one? John asked Erika when he had finished cleaning the dishes and putting everything back in their places. Erika had remained seated at the table staring into the space. Now, she raised her head and shrugged. John held his hand toward her and accompanied her to the living room, where he helped her to sit comfortably on the sofa. Immediately, Erika tucked her legs in and put her arms around them. John crouched down in front of her and gripped her hands.

-Erika, are you all right? This is not like you to be so dejected. I'm starting to worry.

-I'm fine John, just a little tired. That's all. I guess this may be the side effect of time travel. She smiled ruefully.

-Are you sure? Do you want to go back to the hospital for more tests? John asked with an uncertain face.

-I'm sure. And I prefer to be home. I don't mind to be alone either. She ventured.

John gazed intently at her for a while with that odd look that Erika had never seen until now. –Nice try. He said tersely. He rose to his feet and went to choose a movie. Then, he inserted a DVD into the player and sat comfortably beside Erika. Being John, he chose an action movie with lots of stunt acts and car crashes, a good movie nonetheless. Not so long after the movie had begun Erika was soundly asleep.

John watched her with a frown. He was worried about her. This "journey" had taken a toll on her. And she was sleeping too much. That couldn't be normal, no matter what that doctor said. He reached to her and arranged her more comfortably putting her head on his lap. Then, he continued watching the movie.

Some time later, John felt Erika moving restlessly against him and muttering something. She reached with her hand and rested it on his neck, pulling him toward her. The movie had long finished and he had fallen asleep too. Half asleep and half awaken he felt Erika pulled him and instinctively he kissed her. She responded by opening her mouth and letting his tongue inside her mouth. He was holding her head with one arm and with his other hand he reached toward her breasts. He put it under her shirt and with his thumb rubbed her nipple until it was hard. She moaned and called:—Oh, Josh!

-John. He corrected automatically by her mouth and continued kissing her. Suddenly, Erika opened her eyes, realizing she was kissing John. She had been dreaming Josh was holding her and in her dream she had reached toward him. Now, she pushed John and jumped to the other end of the sofa, where she curled up there.

-What do you think you are doing? She asked him in anger. But she was angrier with herself because she had been kissing John and had been enjoying it. Granted, she didn't know it was John until a second ago when she fully woke up, but still. Just yesterday she had been with Josh and today . . .

-I'm sorry Erika. John was real shocked. —I was half asleep and I didn't r . . .

-I think you better leave.

-No!

-John please. I really need to be alone. I have to think . . .

-Fine! I'll go. For a while. But don't you think you can get rid of me so easily. He rose from the sofa, smoothed his clothes, took his car keys and left slamming the door. Erika winced at the sound, but stayed on the sofa. What was it that she had to think? That she was in love with a man that had been dead for almost one hundred and fifty years? That she did not have the slightest idea what could have happened to him? Had he found someone else, after she left? Had he been happy? How long did he live? Did he return to Crawford Fort? Maybe she could look up in the history records to see if he was mentioned anywhere. *Oh Josh! I knew you for so little time!* She thought sighing. *What am I going to do now? Live! Continue living. Move on. I could've stayed with him and I chose not to. So, why am I complaining now? I got what I wanted. My precious project! My wonderful life! I can't regret it now. But I couldn't stay . . . I don't know the effects that would've had. What if I stayed and had children with him? What if for some coincidence they happened to be my own ancestors? No, I don't think that could've happened. Besides, that would've meant I would've ended up being my own creator! That is impossible! It is a time paradox! It was the right thing to do. I did the right thing, what I was supposed to do. But if so, why does it hurt so much? Why? Why I long for his touch, for his breath on my face? Oh Josh! How can I live without you?* Tears were rolling down her face uncontrollably and she put her hands over it giving free rein to her woes.

Some time later, John came back. She hadn't noticed he had taken her keys when leaving earlier. John entered the apartment without making any noise. The place was in shadows, as it had already gotten dark, and all the lights were turned off. He walked quietly through the apartment until he found Erika in her bedroom. She had changed into her pajamas and was curled up on the bed. She hadn't had anything to eat since noon. He was sure because everything in the kitchen was as he had left it. She didn't know it yet but she needed him and he was going to be there for her. He went to the linen closet and got out a set of sheets and a pillow, then went to the sofa, where he took all his clothes off but his trunk shorts and prepared himself to sleep.

John heard some noise and right away opened his eyes. He was a light sleeper. Erika was crying in her sleep. He got up from the couch and stepped into her bedroom. Erika's body was shaking because of the crying. John approached the bed and sat carefully on its side. He shook Erika gently and enfolded her in his arms. Erika snuggled up to him.

-Hush . . . Everything is going to be all right. I have you. John said while he stroked her hair.

-Oh John! She spoke among sobs. –It hurts! It hurts so much . . .

-I know baby, I know. But it will get better, you'll see. He told her tenderly and softly.

-Do you think so? The intelligent and confident Dr. Banner was like a lost child now looking for reassurance.

-I know so, darling. I'll take care of you. I know what you are going through.

-Do you? How could you? It's so strange I don't even understand it myself.

-You wouldn't believe it if I told you. He smiled in the dark with a rueful and somewhat cynical smile that escaped Erika's attention. Not that she would've noticed, she was so engrossed in herself.—Try to sleep now, honey. I'll hold you all night long if I have to.

-Sleep! That's all I seem to do now. But it's the best way not to think, not to remember . . . And she burst in tears again.

-Soon you'll have new memories, happy memories. I promise. And these, the ones that cause you so much pain now will remain treasured but hidden in your mind.

-Would you mind just holding me?

-No. I do it gladly.

-Why?

-'Cause I care about you Erika, don't you know it?

-I guess I do, but now I can't . . . I can't . . .

-Shhhh. It's okay. Don't worry about anything now. Just rest. Tomorrow we'll see. He kissed her tenderly on her forehead and brought her more closely to him, arranging them more comfortable on the bed. Erika gradually calmed down and fell asleep again, while John remained wide-awake thinking and stroking her hair. Finally, John was overcome by sleep as well.

Erika stretched her arm to feel once again the warmness. She had felt secure during the night clinging to John's hard but warm body, feeling his steady heartbeat. She patted the bed but couldn't find it anywhere. *Was I dreaming? Wasn't John here last night? I am not sure what's real and what's a dream these days. They intertwine together.* A sound came from the

bathroom. The shower. *I was not dreaming. John is here!*
She sat upright on the bed. *John! What am I doing?*
-Good morning, Erika. How do you feel today? John
had just stepped out of the bathroom. He had a
small towel wrapped around his hips and his hair was
dripping. Erika could not avoid looking at him. She
had to recognize he was gorgeous. She ogled him from
toe to head. His muscular legs covered by black hair.
His abs, one could count them . . . , his well formed
chest, his strong arms shaped with muscles. He was
muscular but lean. He had an incredible body. That
was so unfair! He was not only strikingly handsome,
but smart, brilliant one would say. And also caring
and nice. She was feeling so lonely now that she had
known true love and had lost it so fast. What she had
known with Josh had lasted so little. She needed to
feel it again. And John was available.

Erika followed the thin line of black hair that
went down his belly into the towel. She also noticed a
bulge protruding from the towel and quickly looked
up to John's face. He was smiling at her, oblivious of
his obvious arousal. The way she had been watching
him! –I hope you don't mind I took a shower. Erika
denied with her head unable to speak. –I'll fix us
some breakfast while you shower and later we can
discuss how we are going to spend the day. I have
some ideas. Erika agreed silently to everything John
said and while he went to dress and prepare breakfast,
she entered the bathroom. Her heart was beating fast
and her breathing was a bit shallow. *How can I have this
reaction to John when I love Josh?* Erika thought while she
bathed. *Lust! Pure lust! I'm a lusty person. Or lonely . . .*
An internal voice said. *The knowledge that you lost Josh*

forever. The bittersweet taste of the ephemeral happiness you knew. Or . . . just plain physical attraction. She finished angrily. *I can't believe it! Get a grip on yourself! Jesus!* She was so disgusted with herself that she finished getting dressed without paying much attention to her appearance. She put on a jean and a loose T-shirt and went to the kitchen.

-So, listen . . . John began while he was serving French toasts on a plate, which he put on the table in front of her. –I was thinking . . . I know the doctor told you to rest but he didn't say you had to stay home all day long. So, I was thinking that maybe we can spend the day out. I'll do the driving and all the stuff so you won't get tired.

-What do you have in mind? Erika asked cautiously.

-We can go to Shoreline Park and have a picnic or if you prefer we can eat something light at the cafeteria there. John said carefully.

-That sounds nice. Erika released the breath she hadn't known she had been holding. She didn't know what she had been expecting but surely not this. This sounded innocent enough, surrounded by people in a public place. The open air could clear her head.

They finished breakfast and arrived at Shoreline Park in fifteen minutes. It was a sunny day with white clouds in a blue sky. The place was already filled with people, laughing children, animated young couples, groups of teenagers . . . *People must be on vacation already.* Erika thought amused.

They went canoeing first, admiring the different kinds of birds that searched for food in the waters. They had a picnic basket with two Italian Panini, some cheese, fresh fruit, and wine that they had gotten at the Lakeside Café. John was rowing sluggishly enjoying the fresh air and the view; once in a while he would glimpse Erika out of the corner of his eye. She seemed relaxed and content. More than in the past couple of days so John was glad with himself that he had invited her to come to the park.

When they were hungry, they approached the shore and set their picnic basket on a tablecloth on the grass. After eating and returning the boat, they decided to go for a walk around the park. By the time they got back to Erika's place it was already dark. John opened the door to Erika's apartment, took Erika's hand, deposited the keys on it and stayed outside. –Aren't you going to come in? She asked perplexed. John had been acting so overprotective since she had gotten back from the past that there was no question in her mind that he would stay for the night again.

-Not tonight. I think you are calmer now and you probably need some time alone. I'll come by tomorrow at 8:30 am to pick you up and take you to the hospital for your checkup. Afterwards if the doctor deems it okay, I'll take you to the lab. The guys have come out with some interesting results.

Erika frowned. That was typical of John, leaving her when she most needed him. First he made himself indispensable and then he would go and . . . *Wow, wow! Stop it right there!* She thought. *When have you become so whiny? He's just behaving like a friend, supportive and caring without suffocating me.*

John grabbed Erika's chin and lifted her head. Unexpectedly he gave her a quick but deep kiss on her mouth. –Good night. I'll see you tomorrow. He turned around and left. *Or . . . he is confusing the hell out of me.* Erika slowly closed the door.

-So, the problem with the coordinates is the number of decimals? That was what sent me to the past instead of to the other side of the country? Erika was astounded.
–And we cannot be certain of the "significant" decimal because it varies from calculation to calculation depending on various factors. We can neither predict the location nor the time because of these variations. There's also a threshold number of decimals under which no teleporting takes place. Erika was pacing back and forth along the lab recapping all the information that her team had collected from her "trip". –However, when you go beyond that significant number of decimals, anything can happen. And you have tried increasing the number of decimals one at a time and you don't know what's occurred. Because in truth, strictly talking, between one number and the next, there's an infinite amount of numbers.
-That's right. Joy took part in Erika's monologue.—We haven't been able to locate the eggs. And the mirror lab definitely has not received any of them. We are positive.

The eggs were the informal way to call the samples they had initially devised to test the teleportation chamber. They were a solid piece of melamine with an ovoid shape, hence the so-called eggs, in different colors to match natural occurring things, such as forest-green, earth-brown, sand-beige, black, or white. The mirror lab was a lab located in the other end of the US at a NASA facility, specifically the Glenn Research Center in Cleveland, Ohio. They were supposed to inform Erika's team of any eggs arrival in the twin chamber located there. This was an important project for NASA for if a living being or a thing could be teleported from one location to another, it would mean that we would not need space ships to travel from one place in the universe to another but we could be able to do it only by teleporting them. This would result in building and fuel costs savings, not experiencing aging for human beings traveling to other planets or galaxies and so forth. It would revolutionize the space missions and the study of the universe and its potential colonization. Now all that seemed in jeopardy at the unexpected discovery of time travel instead. Not that time travel was not something that fascinated every scientific mind in the world but without controlling it, it couldn't be done.

-So, we probably have been spreading eggs all over the ages of time and we can't possibly find out when or where that is. Erika took up again her monologue.

-Mhm. All of them nodded but John, who was deep in thought.

-Well! We seem to find ourselves in crossroads. In two weeks John and I need to inform the board about our progress in the project. I don't need to tell you that should we inform them we are at a dead end they might cut our budget and shut us down. On the other hand, if we tell them about my little adventure, they could shut us down just the same and put other team to investigate these new findings. And I'll be damn if I'm going to handle our two-year work to some new comers with greedy ideas. Besides, I'm not sure how comfortable I feel about time travel, there's so much we don't know, and what if the grandfather paradox is true? We could create chaos. We could destroy ourselves or worst, we could destroy the world as we know it. Damn! I think we all need to think well through this. And I mean all of us, because this is our project and we all have the right to an opinion. I say we call it off the day and go home to consider things, pros and cons. Anyhow, we will continue working with what we have so far for these next two weeks. We will review every piece of data we got. We will check everything once more. And by the time the board meeting takes place, we'll have a sound position to inform.

Erika finished and turned to look at John for the first time since their arrival at the lab. He had come punctually to pick her up at her place and take her to the hospital. Patiently, he had waited outside the doctor's office. When Erika had come out, he had driven her to the lab where he instructed the team to bring her up to date, after she had informed him that the doctor had cleared her. All of that with so much as two or three words, the necessary "Good morning", "let's go", "are you ready?" stuff. –John, did you plan to give me a ride home? Or should I call a taxi? The doctor said I'm fine and I can drive by myself tomorrow. She sounded so professional, she thought proud of herself.

-Of course I'll take you. Give me a minute to turn the computer off. He passed a hand through his hair messing it up. He looked tired. Erika realized with surprise. She had been so self-absorbed these past few days that she hadn't thought of anyone else but herself.

-John . . . I wanted to thank you for taking care of me and for being so patient with me these last days. She said gently.

-It's okay. That's what friends are for, isn't it? He smiled ruefully.

Friends? Friends? No, not really, those kisses were anything but friendly. That weird look you direct to me since I'm back is anything but friendly. The way you've been taking care of me or holding me seems everything but friendly. But hey! What do I know? That was what Erika wanted to shout at him, but she didn't. She just played it in her mind and said nothing. 'Cause she really didn't know what she would achieve by saying it. Hell! She didn't even know if she wanted to go deep into that! She was more confused by the minute. She was certain she loved Josh. But she had a little suspicion that she was starting to feel love for John too. Not friendly or sisterly love but love, love. And how could she feel love for two men at the same time? That was impossible! She had always despised those women that pretended to be in love with two men at the same time and claimed that if was out of their control. And she also felt a pang of guilt and betrayal toward Josh. It doesn't matter that the man had been dead for almost one century and a half. She loved him and she could not betray him like that. Not so soon anyway. *There must be a decent period for mourning a lost love.* She thought in anguish. Then, she almost gave a guffaw. *Man! I'm starting to sound like a soap opera heroine.*

The next two weeks were a hard period. They went all over the data they had once and again and they continued testing. The eggs kept disappearing but the mirror lab kept getting none of them. Who knows where or better yet "when" the eggs were scattered. Not knowing for sure how to control the dates or places of arrival, none of them thought it safe for one of them to test travel. After all, Erika's destination had been totally random as far as they were concerned. They weren't sure they could replicate it and they hadn't been able to retrieve any of the samples, so how they had been able to get her back was becoming a mystery for them. Finally, they gathered all the data, put them in order, and stopped further testing. It was the day previous to the meeting before the board and Erika was gathering her belongings when John approached her. He had been working as hard as every one of them, if not harder and they had shared only job related topics.

-Erika, can I come by your place later? There's something I need to tell you. John told her serious.

-Sure. Erika replied surprised.

-I'll see you later then. John said and then left the lab.

Some time later, Erika was making some tea. She had to make some decisions and prepare mentally for the meeting the next day. She hadn't even had time to change her clothes, so she was still wearing her suit skirt and her blouse. The doorbell rang and there it was John. He hadn't changed his work clothes either.

-John. Come in. Erika invited him after opening the door. John stepped in and closed the door but remained there.

-I'm leaving. He said without inflexion in his voice.

-What? You're leaving? You're just gonna walk out on me like that? Erika asked taken aback. –I don't believe this. I just can't believe it! She moved her head from side to side.

-Don't worry. I'll leave after the meeting. You don't have to fret about . . .

-The meeting doesn't worry me. I can handle it. She interrupted angrily. –So, you are sure what's going to happen tomorrow? It was more a statement than a question.

-Aren't you? Do you think anyone in the team is going to act differently?

-No, but still. For fairness I need to hear what they have to say before I inform it to the board. But, where are you going? Why are you leaving? Why are you walking out on me? She repeated.—How can you walk away from us?

-Us? What us? John frowned. –There is no us. There never was. You wouldn't let to be an us. He said angrily.

-How can you say that? What about the past few days? There's something going on between us. Don't deny it. She counterattacked irately.

-What are you talking about? He replied annoyed.—Every time that I have tried to come closer to you, you have pushed me away. You are driving me crazy! One minute you look at me as if you wanted to eat me and the next, you look at me as if I could eat you. Literally! Eat you! Horrified! One minute you look at me with tenderness and the next like you would kill me.

-Well, you're no angel either. You treated me with care and tenderness the week after my . . . my . . . experience and then, suddenly you turn into an ice cube, all business. She shouted at him.

-That's because I was trying to control myself! He shouted back. –I needed to concentrate on the job. If I think about you I get distracted. You don't know how hard it's been to me these last two years. Always behaving carefully around you, always keeping control.

-And why you have to be so controlled all the time? She yelled even higher if that was possible.

-So, I won't lift you in my arms, take you to the bedroom, and make love to you like a madman. That's why! Because his voice was deeper he could not reach the altos that she did.

-And why don't you? What are you waiting for? That I fall on my knees and beg you to make love to me? Is that what is going to take? After the words had come out of her mouth, she realized what she had just said. She had recognized that she wanted to make love to him. Was that true? She didn't have time to reconsider. John had been on the verge of replying something but he closed his mouth and stared at her for a few seconds. Then he lifted her in his arms and kissed her hard and hungrily on her mouth. For a minute Erika thought about Josh and the wonderful but short love they had shared. *He would understand. He would want me to be happy. I must move on.* For a brief moment she doubted but then surrendered to John's kiss, the warm and delicious sensation of his tongue inside her mouth. The strong arms that were holding her and the hard chest against she was being held. She raised her arms to surround John's neck and returned the kiss with all the passion she was capable of. It seemed that was the signal John had been waiting for. In that instant he strode to her bedroom but deposited her gently on the bed. He looked intently at Erika.

-Tonight, there will be only us in the bedroom. No one else. I, John, will make love to you.

He kicked out his shoes and without even taking his clothes off he laid on the bed beside Erika. He continued kissing her deeply while pushing up Erika's skirt with his hands with brusque movements. Next he tore her panties with a single tug and then he lowered his zipper. His penis came out rigid and without waiting a second longer, he introduced it inside Erika with a hard and long thrust. She was ready for him, wet and warm inside. He moved over her like a mad man, as he had well expressed minutes earlier, but Erika didn't mind. She was as anxious as he. In a few strokes they both reached the orgasm, in an explosion of sensations. Erika just a minute ahead of John.

When it was all over, John collapsed over her. –I'm sorry. He was still breathing fast. –The next time will be better, I promise. He tried to rise himself but Erika stopped him.

-No, please don't get up. Stay.

-Okay, but if I fall asleep don't blame me later. He warned her.

-I won't, but just hold me. John did as told. He arranged himself slightly to the side so he would not be too heavy on her. And he held her. They both dozed for a while until Erika felt John's organ starting to get hard again.

-Let me do it right this time, darling. John told Erika with a deep voice.

-I don't know that you can beat that first time. It was incredible to me. She answered.

-I'll try. He separated from her body and slowly took out each piece of clothing one at a time. Every time he took something he would caress her and kiss her all over her body leaving a warm trace. When Erika was completely naked, he took his own clothes, faster this time. He admired her body while touching her all over. Then he devoted his attention to certain areas of the body with his hands and mouth. First, her neck, then her breasts and from there he followed a path down her stomach to her legs. At first he ignored her intimate parts concentrated on touching and kissing her legs. But as he went up them he became more interested in the center of her pleasure. Erika was out of control at the way he was making love to her, she pulled his hair and implored him to enter. He did. Slowly at first, only tempting her but soon the game turned against him and he had to increase the speed and the depth of his thrusts. They reached the orgasm almost in unison again. They slept holding each other. Just before dawn, John woke Erika up with small kisses and caresses. This time they made love slowly and tenderly, both taking time to touch and feel the other. After that, exhausted they fell asleep until Erika's alarm went on.

-What do you say if a take a quick shower, get dress real fast, and then we both go to your place. You shower too and change clothes. After our meeting we go back to your place or mine, whichever you prefer, and make love again until we get so tired that we forget all about the meeting. Erika suggested while John got dressed and she was on her way to the bathroom.

-I'd say that's the best idea you've had in years. He went to her and caught her before she could enter the bathroom. He kissed her deeply and gave her a soft pat on the butt. Then he went to the kitchen to make some coffee. By the time she appeared in the kitchen, fresh from the shower and ready to leave, he was eating his second pop tart. She drank a cup of coffee and they left for John's place.

The meeting was held at a different building. One full with offices and rooms like the one where the meeting was taking place. After the whole teleporting team had discussed each point of view and had reached an agreement, John and Erika went to meet their evaluation board. Those were the ones who could start up and shut down projects, the ones who assigned allocations, budgets, and appointed the people to work on the projects. Yes, they were God! The ones with the power. Or so they thought. But not really since they did not know all the details like in this case.

-So, you are telling us that you have not been able to teleport anything so far. Madam chairman was addressing John and Erika after they had reported their results.

-That's right. The samples just disintegrate in the air without leaving any trace. Erika agreed. –They never reappear.

-But how can you be so sure of this? Another member asked.

-Well, we really can't. For all that we know, they could be lying on the desert or in someone's backyard across the country or all over the world. But the fact is that they haven't appeared in the mirror lab or at any other of our facilities. –John backed up Erika. He was in the meeting really to support her, since Erika was the team's leader.

-The point is, Erika continued,—that we haven't been able to control the materialization, which is the prime objective of the project. If we can't control it that means we cannot send anybody anywhere.

-And you are saying that you can't achieve the project objective. Another member intervened.

-Not with the technology available, we can't. Perhaps in a few years. But we certainly don't want to continue expending money on something that is not producing results, when we could be using it for more urgent matters.

-That is for this board to decide Dr. Banner. The madam chairman replied.

-Certainly! Nonetheless, should we decide to cut your budget or shut down your project, both you and every member of your team will retain you salary and benefits until a new project suitable for you is found. We regard you and your team as highly qualified scientists. You have nothing to worry about.

-Thank you, sir. Erika addressed the old man that had spoken last. He was a bright scientist himself and a very fair person.

-Well, we'll let you know our decision as soon as we can. Thank you Dr. Banner. Thank you Dr. McMahon.

Back in the lab, Erika and John shared the news with her team.

-So, you think they're really going to shut us down? Joy asked half hoping that wouldn't happen.

-I'm afraid so, Joy. We have been working for two years and haven't really provided reliable results. Unless you count my experience as a result. Or as reliable.

And we all agreed that was not a result we wanted to share. At least not at this time. Erika said.

-Yes, no matter our reasons, that in the end turned out to be quite different, more than I expected, we all agreed that the world is not ready yet to travel in time. Mark commented.

-Yeah. Least of all the government. Those sob's would use temporal travel for warfare for sure and they could kill my next to be fiancé. Luke added. He was always making jokes and comments that not everybody could understand. But he was a very good scientist and a nice person.

-Luke, you should be careful with what you say. Someday someone is going to hear you and they are going to kick your ass out of here. Joy warned him.

-I'd like to see that. I'd sue everybody in here. Last time I checked we live in a democracy and I have the right to say what I think. Luke replied half serious, half joking. As always.

-Yeah, stick to the Fifth Amendment. Mark said joking too.

-I sure like to see that one, I mean your ass being kicked out. Not a pretty sight, I'm afraid. John added. And all of them laughed.

The letter arrived three days later. An unusually fast response for the board. They usually took more than a week, but someone must have decided that they had spent too much money on that project in particular. John and Erika were at his place. They had made love after toasting with champagne to the loss of their jobs. They didn't have the slightest

idea of what they were going to do next. They had
been making love every night since that first night.
John was an attentive but passionate lover and Erika
found herself in love with him. How she could love
him and Josh was out of her understanding. And
though she still missed Josh she was happy with John.
However she didn't know what was going to happen
with them now that they were both out of job. John
turned toward Erika and looked her in the eye. –I
love you. He said in a husky voice. This was the first
time John told her that he loved her and Erika felt
overwhelmed. But before she could say anything,
John got out of the bed and went to his closet. There,
he went through one of the drawers and took out
a parcel. He stood there for a moment holding the
package and then turned around and walked back to
the bed. He sat there and offered the parcel to Erika.
What Erika thought at first a paper wrapping turned
out to be an animal skin, leather. She unwrapped
it and found two different bundles, one small and
unevenly shaped, the other flat. She unwrapped the
leather of the flat one and stunned saw there were
some folded paper sheets inside. They looked old
and yellowish. When she turned them she went even
more staggered at seeing her name written on it.
She looked at John who had been quietly seated in
front of her and he nodded encouraging her to open
it. She read: "To Dr. Erika Banner, PhD in Physics.
NASA's Ames Research Center, California. To be
delivered after July 24, 2010." She carefully unfolded
the letter inside the outer paper sheet with her name
and read.

Dakota Territory, September 3, 1866

My beloved Erika,

Much time has passed since I met you. But I want you to know that I have always loved you and I will love you until the day I die. I believe that my days are soon going to come to an end. So I want you to know what happened to me after you left. Or I should say disappeared in a sphere of light until there was nothing more than a dot and then nothing. I believe that you will read this letter in a very far away day. I also believe that we will find each other again in your time. But I want you to know I have been happy. I know you need to know this. Don't ask me how, I just know. There are a lot of things about you that to this day I still don't understand and I don't intend to. However, as some of the things you talked about have become true, I am convinced you and I will see each other again. I look forward to it. Well, I think I'm raving so I'll go on with my story.

As you disappeared into thin air on that afternoon, I fell on my knees, holding your watch. I haven't parted from it until now, when I'm turning it with this letter for you to have. As you said, it stopped after a couple of years following your departure. I could never get it to work again, but I kept it always with me.

I stayed there numb for I don't know how much time not believing that I wouldn't see you anymore. See, I wasn't looking for a relationship when I found you but you got inside my skin and I fell deeply in love with you. So, I couldn't believe my luck, why had I found you to loose you in so a short time? It seemed like a joke from the universe. A big joke on me. Now, I understand what you told me before you left, that you felt a pull to go back. If you hadn't, none of what happened next would've occurred. Anyhow, I got up after a while. My knees hurt, but I didn't pay attention to it. I went to the bonfire and I drank some cold coffee. With what was left I put out the fire. I left everything there. I went to the horses and untied them. I tied yours to mine. I mounted and let the horses went wherever they wanted to go. I figured they would go back to the fort. I really didn't care where they took me. The horses wandered for several days, I can't remember how many. But they never got near the fort. Sometimes, they would stop to drink water from a creek; sometimes I dismounted and drank some too. Others I stayed on the horse letting them quench their thirst. I grew weak from lack of food and so little water. Gradually I think I must have developed a fever because I started to have hallucinations. I would see you smiling at me, calling my name. In a moment of clarity, I tied myself to the horse so I continued to be on it. Eventually, after several days, the horses arrived to an Indian settling. I didn't realize it, I was so out in my hallucinations by then. The horses stopped there. It was like something or someone had been pulling them to that place and when they arrived they didn't wander anymore. Someone pulled me out of the horse and put me inside a tipi. There, someone gave me something to drink, first water, then a concoction. I was delirious for the next several days. Afterwards, they told me they didn't think I would make it.

It wasn't my time then however. Two people took care of me during those days. An Indian woman called Anpaytoo and Anna. Imagine the coincidence, I ended up in Anna's husband's camp! Anyway, as Anpaytoo's fiancée had been killed in Anna's retrieval, she offered to take care of the white man. She saw it as a way to give some goodness instead of retribution. And besides, she was lonely. But the first time I looked into her eyes, I mean the first time I wasn't feverish or delirious, I saw you. I saw your soul. In her beautiful brown eyes I saw your look. I know you probably think I'm talking nonsense because I'm old. But it's true. That's why you had to go back. There couldn't be two of you at the same time. And as my adopted people, the Sioux, I believe we reincarnate in the vicinities of our family.

Continuing with my story . . . As I began to recover, I could see more of you in Anpaytoo. Although she behaved as a truly Sioux woman, she had the strength of character and the fortitude that you have. Gradually, without realizing it, I found myself in love with her. It was odd the fact of being aware that I was in love with two women at the same time, you and Anpaytoo. Now I can understand it better. Now that I'm old and I have lived more. But by that time I felt like I was betraying you. As time passed though, I also fell in love with the way of living and the costumes of the Sioux. I asked Chetan, Anna's husband to allow me to stay with them. To become one of them. As I realized that you weren't coming back, I also asked him permission to marry Anpaytoo if she would have me. It turned out that her first engagement had been arranged for both her family and the boyfriend's family. So, even though she had cared for him and she had been sad to learn that he died, she hadn't loved him. But oh surprise! She loved me. She said later on that she had fallen for the white man the first time she saw me, almost dead.

So, I married her and we have been very happy together. She is a wonderful woman. How can't she be? She is you and you are her. I'm convinced now. When I told her about you, she told me that maybe you and her *were the same in different times. What I can tell you is that every time I made love to her, it was like I made love to you. The same feelings, the same passion, the same love. We had three children. Two boys and a girl. I will pass this letter to my first boy so he passes it on to his first son or daughter, so he or she passes it on in turn to his/her first son or daughter until it reaches you. So you know how much I loved you during all my life and that I never forgot about you, my love.*

I didn't want to say good-bye without telling you that Anna has been very happy with Chetan too. Besides their first son, they had three more children: Another boy and two girls. Their oldest son married my daughter. And my oldest son married their oldest daughter. I now have ten grandchildren ranging from ages 6 to 18 years old. I stayed with the Sioux. I became one of them and never returned to the white people. I found the Sioux life better suited for me.

I return your watch to you with this letter, trusting that it will arrive shortly after our encounter (for you) so you live your life happily and without remorse. I know I'll see you again in your time, my love. Wait for me.

I'll love you for eternity.
Josh McMahon.

A tear fell on the letter smudging some of the words. Erika was crying and she hadn't noticed it. She opened the other bundle and found her watch. It had stopped at 12:38 pm. It looked old but one could see it was well taken care of. She lifted her head and found John looking at her with a serious expression. He had not uttered a word while she had been reading the letter.

-You're Josh's descendant! Erika told him.

-Yes! I'm his great-great-great-great-grandson.

-Do you think that you and him . . . ?

-If we are the same person? If we share the same soul?
I don't know Erika. My scientific mind doesn't believe
in that. But my Indian heritage had taught me to
believe in reincarnation. I can tell you this though.
The first time I saw you, I was drawn to you. That's
why I requested to be in your project.

-You requested to be in my project? Why?

That was not all John had done. He had also
declined to lead his own project to be under Erika's
leadership, but he didn't tell her that. –I don't
exactly know. It was something in the spurt of the
moment. Once I saw you I couldn't let you go. I told
you something attracted me to you. So I asked you
out but you said you didn't get involved in personal
affairs with your co-workers.

-I thought you wanted a meaningless relationship and
I had recently got out of a painful one with another
co-worker. Afterwards, when I saw all the bimbos'
parade I was sure I had made the right decision.

-Yeah. Well. I was trying to get you out of my system.

-And when did you get Josh's letter? Erika changed
the subject. She was curious to know how the letter
had ended up in John's hands.

-It was a year ago. On my father's 70 birthday. He
called me apart and handed it to me. He said he was
getting too old and as his oldest son I needed to fulfill
Josh's wishes. He said that it was a coincidence that I
work at the same place where the letter was addressed.
And that the time of the letter was getting close. He
said to look for you after July 24, 2010 and give it

to you. I couldn't believe it when I saw your name on it. I asked him if he knew what its contents were and he answered no. He hadn't looked because it was addressed to you. On the contrary, when I got home that day, I opened it and read it. I didn't understand how that could have happened. It involved you traveling in time. But how? We weren't working on that, we were working in teleporting. Then I saw the watch and the next day I noticed that you carried the same watch. That meant that you had had to travel to his time between that moment and the date of the delivery. I didn't know what to do. On one hand, I didn't know if I wanted you to travel in time. We don't know the repercussions that can have. Except in this case I knew. What if you traveled to his time and somehow you prevented him from getting married to Anpaytoo, my great-great-great-great-grandmother? What if you didn't show here anymore? I mean, there is no proof in the letter that you really came back here at all. So I spent a hellish year waiting to see what happened seizing between telling you before it happened or not. Then, that Monday on July 17, when you couldn't be found anywhere; when we discovered you have been teleported to someplace by mistake, I knew. I knew you have traveled to his time. That you were there. And I knew that you would fall in love with him. And I didn't know for sure if you would be back. So I became a wreck and a tyrant. I was jealous of Josh for having you and also worried sick that you wouldn't come back. I made the team work day and night to bring you back. I yelled at them, insulted them. I don't even know how they speak to me. Perhaps because they knew I was so worried. Then, when I had lost all hope to find you, when I thought I lost you forever, you appeared. That was why I was so out of control the days afterwards, that was why I kissed you. I was half crazed.

-Now I get your odd look. You knew. You knew and that is why you watched me with that strange look.

-I was basically jealous that you were in love with him and not with me. And also, you were suffering and I hurt for you. I love you with all my heart Erika, with all my soul. I have been in love with you for two years. I don't know if my soul is Josh's soul. But I can tell you that the first time we made love, well, the second one really, 'cause the first one I was in a hurry, it was as if we had made love before. I knew how and where to touch you, what you liked most. It was as if somehow I remembered.

-I know what you mean. Every time you kissed me, even though it was different, it was so familiar. That's why I confused you with Josh those first times you kissed me. I really understand what he expresses in the letter, when he says that making love to Anpaytoo was like making love to me. There is a familiarity between us John. Something that it was there before we made love that first time. I love you. You, John. This you, the current and actual you. And though I hope with all my heart that we really reincarnate and all that stuff is true, and though I love Josh and I will never stop loving him, I love you just the same or even more. She finished with tears still rolling down her face.

-Would you then like to share the rest of this life with me? John asked her with wet eyes.

-Yes John, I would. She grinned. And then, they made love again slowly and passionately.

EPILOGUE

-Mommy, can I wear an Indian princess custom for Halloween? Winona, their six year old asked Erika.

-Sure honey. Is grandma going to sew the dress? Erika asked her daughter while continued working on the dinner preparations.

-Yes! She told me she is going to make such a beautiful dress that I'm going to look just as a real princess.

-You don't look Indian, with your blonde hair and your green eyes. Chenoa, her other daughter, replied.

-Like you do? You have blue eyes! Winona told her.

-I look after daddy. Isn't it daddy? Chenoa looked at her father for confirmation.

-You're both Indian princesses. It's just there is white man's blood running through your veins too. John tried to explain to both of her daughters. He was helping with the dinner.

-We know, 'cause of mommy! Both girls said in unison.

-And because of a great-great-great-great-great-grandfather who was also white. That's why your father has blue eyes. Erika intervened again.

-So, we get to be real Indian princesses although our skin is fairer than daddy's? Chenoa asked again.

-You get to be whatever you want. You have a great heritage, American Indian and Scottish and some other European, which I don't recall. Now, go play while mommy and I finish fixing dinner.

The girls went running and laughing to the playroom. Erika approached John after the girls left and told him in his ear. –After we have dinner and tuck the girls in, what do you say if we try to make an Indian warrior?

-I'll hurry. John answered gulping and half closing his eyes with that bright look in them. Erika laughed and they kissed.

THE END